The Refugee

The Refugee

Nikhil Khasnabish

BLACK EAGLE BOOKS
Dublin, USA | Bhubaneswar, India

Black Eagle Books
USA address:
7464 Wisdom Lane
Dublin, OH 43016

India address:
E/312, Trident Galaxy, Kalinga Nagar,
Bhubaneswar-751003, Odisha, India

E-mail: info@blackeaglebooks.org
Website: www.blackeaglebooks.org

First International Edition Published by
Black Eagle Books, 2023

THE REFUGEE
by **Nikhil Khasnabish**
Email: nabish_328@rediffmail.com
Cell: 9101141113

Cover & Interior Design: Ezy's Publication

ISBN- 978-1-64560-423-5 (Paperback)
Library of Congress Control Number: 2023945428

Printed in the United States of America

for the riot victims and refugees

1

1964

Every year in December, after the harvest had been gathered, the Hindu peasants of Munsiganj used to celebrate *nabanna*. At *nabanna*, all the members of the Hindu families were invited to Gunen's house.

To help Meghna, Gunen's wife, some women busied themselves with cleaning up with bamboo brooms. Some carried water from the pond while some mopped the courtyard and the floors of the houses. Drinking water was brought from the well and tanks were filled. The women, who were adept at dancing and singing, rehearsed in the outhouse, shutting the doors and windows so that none could disturb them. Two women, Gunen addressed as *kaki-ma* (auntie), engaged admiration for drawing motif in the courtyard with rice powder coloured in various colours.

In Gunen's house, the *nabanna* feast had always been better than in other peasants' houses. No families could break the record Meghna had set. Like in other years, that year too, Meghna's cakes and rice pudding became a talk, and Gunen was sure it'd linger till next year.

Gunen and Meghna were born and brought up in

the two separate villages in the district of Mymensingh, and they spoke the common Bengali dialect of the district. They'd never gone to school and didn't feel ashamed of admitting that they were illiterate.

Their home comprised two small houses they used for themselves and guests, a kitchen, a cow house, a store house, an outhouse, and a granary. The roofs of all the houses were built with corrugated tin sheets except the roofs of the cow house. The roofs of the cow house were built with grass. Thatched bamboos were used for building the walls of all the houses. In response to necessity, the walls were repaired or replaced after examining the walls' resistance and presence of termites. Special attention was given to the granary walls. Failing to enter the granary through the wooden door, the big rats made holes in the walls by sitting on the horizontal bamboo bars supporting the structure. They ate a lot of paddies. In response to time and need, all the walls were scrubbed with cow dung.

'*Gobar gorome ghar thanda rakhe aar shite gorom*', Meghna used to say in Bengali dialect of Mymensingh, after scrubbing the walls with cow dung. ('*Cow dung keeps a house cool in summer and warm in winter.*')

Gunen was of medium build, strong and sturdy, and brown-complexioned, his face neither round nor long. He was clean-shaven. Since she'd picked a crust of milk from his moustache, he had never let his moustache work as a filter. As an orphan, he'd been raised at his maternal uncles' at Pipradanga, six miles from Munsiganj, his village.

Gunen had objected to his marriage at twenty-one. He'd planned to marry after buying eight *bighas* of land to add to his father's eight *bighas* so he could feel comfortable with his property and live like a rich man at Munsiganj. But everything had moved in a reverse direction when he had been forced to see Meghna, a nineteen-year-old piece of beauty. Throwing a sly glance at his maternal uncle, the instant he'd nodded his head and let his smiling eyes negotiate with hers and get locked, his maternal uncle had not wasted a minute to say yes to the proposal to the pleasure of both the families.

Gunen hadn't taken dowry. But he'd gladly accepted the wooden chest gifted by his father-in-law. They considered the chest their most precious property.

In the first year of their marriage, Gunen and Meghna became parents of a son they named Gyanpada Sarkar Ginu. She again became pregnant when Ginu was two years old.

*

The *nabanna* feast was over around two hours ago, and all the invitees had left except Taimoor Ali, who hadn't moved from the chair on the veranda since he'd sat in it. He smoked cigarettes one after another and ogled Meghna, smiling his nasty smile, whenever she came out of the kitchen and went to the main house to put the utensils back in the chest.

'The courtyard is waiting to be cleaned up, Taimoor. Dusk will fall after an hour. How long will you keep sitting here? I think you'd better go home now,' Gunen said, looking at the slanting sun.

Taimoor laughed out loud. He lit another cigarette, gave a long drag on it, leaned back in the chair, and propped up his legs against the veranda post in front of him. 'We're friends. I'll forever remember Meghna's cakes and rice pudding. I won't go home without eating some more cakes and pudding.'

'I didn't invite you.'

'I'm your *dosto*. I've the right to attend a feast at my *dosto's*, uninvited. I've the right to sit if I want to.' Taimoor blew out the smoke and laughed louder than before. '*Dosto* means friend. I told you I'd teach you and Meghna English. Say when I can start.' He wiped his lips on the backs of his hands and smiled. 'My bad luck I couldn't see Meghna before her marriage.'

'You're a beast. You're nothing but a beast. I'll always call you a beast.'

'How can a kafir call me a beast? I'm Chairman Arif Ali's son. You know that. And you also know people swallow thrice before looking at my eyes. It's your good luck you're my *dosto*.' Taimoor spat his paan-juice upstream on the side of the veranda and wiped the trickling juice the wind had blown to his cheek. He lifted the chair, dropped it. Then he sat down, lit another cigarette, gave a long drag on it, and the smoke he habitually blew through his protruding lips faintly clouded Gunen's stare. 'I'll set fire to your house if you again call me a beast.' He stared at the glowing point of the cigarette, and then, laughing like a villain, he spat the paan juice on the veranda wall Meghna had scrubbed with raw cow dung early in the morning.

Gunen thoughtfully focused on Taimoor's atrocity constituting provocation. Taimoor wouldn't find an escape route, if Gunen erupted like a volcano. Taimoor had ogled Meghna since he'd first seen her. Not caring his warning and request and her severe objections, Taimoor had often looked for chances to talk dirty.

Meghna came out from inside the kitchen, slightly bowed to him, and spliced her hands at her chest. 'Please leave us to ourselves. We feel disturbed.'

Taimoor stood up and walked over to her, wearing his nasty smile, and then as soon as he touched her cheek, Gunen decided not to allow the Taimoor to cross the limits anymore; he'd already crossed the limits beyond tolerance. So anger boiling in his head, as he flew into his room and came back with his dagger, he saw Taimoor laughing and struggling with her trying desperately to prevent his hands from touching her breasts. Not wasting a split second to think if he should attack Taimoor, he let loose his rage Taimoor failed to overcome despite putting up the best efforts. Then, before he could strike Taimoor's right forearm, Taimoor stepped back, and he lowered the dagger, his focus on the blood on Taimoor's left forearm Taimoor pressed to stop the blood flow. Taimoor wiped the wound with his handkerchief, smelled the blood, and spread the handkerchief to show them the stains. Taimoor looked bewildered, his mouth moving like that of a fish out of water.

'Meghna will wash this handkerchief,' Taimoor said when he came back to normal, after a few seconds.

'I'll send the dagger into your belly if you delay here even a minute,' Gunen said, the dagger in his hand at the level of Taimoor's belly.

Taimoor, the putz, who seemed to have failed to sense Gunen's disdain raining on his face, snickered, took a currency note from the right side pocket of his kurta, and thrust it into Gunen's hand. 'Buy toys for Ginu with this gift of one hundred taka.'

Without a word, Gunen tore the note into pieces and hurled them to the raw cow dung heaped up near the pomegranate tree to scrub the courtyard next morning.

Taimoor stepped close to Gunen. 'You bloody son-of-a-kafir. I'll crush your bones if you fail to stand corrected.'

Throwing an angry look at Taimoor's contorted face that looked more despicable, Gunen scooped the raw cow dung with his right hand and threw it into Taimoor's face so hard Taimoor's face got ignominiously soiled. With a violent jerk of the head, Taimoor gripped Gunen's neck and, by wrenching his head into a reverse position, gave him the feeling of being strangled. Before Taimoor could succeed in using more violence, Gunen collected whatever strength he could and continued struggling until he could manoeuvre his neck free from Taimoor's grip. Gunen punched Taimoor's belly, and Taimoor bent double to retard more punches. Then, the moment Taimoor failed to resist the impact of Gunen's kicks and looped down on his bottom, Gunen felt Maghna's hands arrest his from behind and pull him hard back so that Taimoor, torn from Gunen's grip, stood aloof, defeated.

'Don't dare to come to our house again. Next time, I won't let you return home. You were never my *dosto*. You are not my *dosto*. You're a beast. You're my enemy. My enemy can never be my *dosto*,' Gunen said in a tone of severe warning.

'If I fail to marry Meghna, I'll set fire to your house

and throw you out of Munsiganj.' Taimoor smiled his nasty smile.

After Taimoor had stalked out of the compound, with a violent gait, his father's gift, Meghna poured water on the stains of blood on the veranda and purified the place with raw cow dung from near the pomegranate tree.

*

Meghna sat beside Gunen silently sitting on the bench, leaning his head against the veranda wall. Glancing at the room, where Ginu was sleeping, oblivious to the melodrama in their compound, Gunen looked at Meghna: she looked distant, a coil of fear like a python likely to wake up from its slumber to stir into action to its necessity any moment in her eyes; her deep breathing heaved her chest. She had become more beautiful after Ginu's birth. He stood up, fingered her unkempt hair before running his fingers over the remains of Taimoor's blows on his swollen lips and on his face, and thought more fight would've given him the real satisfaction he needed to feel his anger melt away.

'Don't fear him, Meghna. I'm with you.' He flopped on the dirt floor of the veranda, the dagger in his hand and his mind floating in the stream of thoughts he had no control over.

Arif Ali considered himself as the most powerful man and abased the Hindus as slaves though they had voted for him. A year ago, he'd married a girl, who was his elder daughter's age. The Hindus, the victims of bigotry, couldn't stand united and protest about his biasness and injustice. They remained in constant fear of robbers and thieves. The women couldn't move freely. They were teased and followed. Like a pack of hyenas, uncertainties haunted the families of beautiful young women and girls and disturbed their sleep. The broken pieces of the Hindu dreams had lain scattered here and there in the village corners. To get rid of the curse of living as Hindus in East Pakistan, they had only one option and that was to leave for India, where he assumed they'd be able to live like humans without fear and subjugation. But next moment when he thought that East Pakistan wasn't Arif Ali's father's country and it belonged to all, he resolved to motivate the Hindus to fight for equal rights, not yielding to injustice.

2

Gunen woke up to the shouts and cries. He took his dagger from under the mattress and carefully got out of bed so that Ginu and Meghna didn't wake up. Before taking the lock and key from the peg, he stood in the middle of the room, for a few seconds. He soundlessly opened the door and sneaked out. He locked the door from the outside and put the key under the chair.

He went to the front yard and listened to the noises. They were coming from the direction of the Python Bridge.

It was a small wooden bridge over the Python Marsh. It connected the eastern and western parts of the road the British had failed to build. Flood waters had broken the road whenever they'd tried to build it.

A pair of male and female pythons lived in the marsh. They ambushed their prey on the bridge, especially at night. In the rain, they rested on the bridge. The python couple used to force their babies to live elsewhere, but no one knew where that elsewhere was. The pythons had eaten up many people, swallowed many goats, and dogs. At night, people never dared to cross the bridge alone, and while crossing the bridge, they shone torches the pythons were known to be afraid of.

Gafur, Gunen's farmhand and friend, was more courageous than Gunen, and he ignored those stories. To cross the bridge at night, he neither shone a torch nor carried a lantern; he struck the planks with his lathi.

Gunen ran fast to get to where the crowd was. A goon was pointing his dagger to Purbash Das's daughter Tuhina's belly and dragging her along a narrow dirt path towards the Brahmaputra. Tuhina was desperately putting up defence and crying for help. Gunen threw himself between Tuhina and the goon. Gunen's involvement offered impetus to Purbash Das, who was struggling to free her from the goon's hands; Purbash Das became as ferocious as the other Muslim and Hindu neighbours fighting to overpower the other five goons armed with swords and daggers. With his dagger, Gunen discharged a blow on the goon's wrist, and the goon let go of her hand to fight with Gunen. Then, finally, failing to combat the villagers charging at them with lathis and big machetes, called *ramdao*, and spears, the goons admitted defeat and scattered towards the Python Bridge.

Gunen ran back home faster than before. He washed the dagger, kept it on the bench. After washing his hands and feet, he sprayed water on his face and dried his face and hands and feet on the *gamchcha* from the clothesline on the western side of the veranda. He picked up the key, opened the door. Then, the dagger in his right hand, he sneaked into the room like he'd sneaked out. He climbed into bed. Meghna and Ginu were in sound sleep; she was snoring rhythmically, and his hands were around her neck. Having a look at the ancestral dagger, preserved like a precious treasure and a symbol of protection, he examined its sharpness and snipped the left thumb ball on its blade and a few drops of blood stained the bedspread despite his pressing the thumb to stem the blood. To hide the stains from Meghna, who, he knew, would pester him with questions if she happened to discover the stains, he folded the bedspread on his side right away and decided to wash it himself. He sent the dagger to its place, then lay down.

3

As usual, just getting up, Gunen went straight to the cow house to look at the hooves of the brown cow Meghna most cared for.

'Always take a look at the hooves of a cow, just getting up,' Meghna had said.

When he didn't see the cow in the cow house, he first surveyed the stubble fields within the range of his eyes— the clear view of the fields was blurred by the fog—and then, not finding her in the fields he'd walked into, he searched for her in back of the outhouse, in the backyard, in the orchard, and at the patch of grass down the dyke of the pond before standing under the mango tree on the pond's bank.

Had she been stolen?

Gunen sat down, leaned back against the rough trunk of the tree, and spread his legs on the dew-drenched grass, his look at the pond, where five-to-six-foot-deep water remained even in March when water went down in others' ponds. Almost at regular intervals, the fish rose and broke the rhythms of the ripples. In this pond, he remembered, he had taught Meghna how to swim, how they had made swimming competitions when they had got into the pond together, and how he had always let her excel so she could build her confidence in her ability to swim like him. Lifting his eyes from the pond, he looked towards the fruit trees in the compound. He had to buy only oranges for them; they fed orange peels to the cows; Meghna fed her peels to the brown cow, which was given special attention because of being pregnant.

Since that day, Meghna hadn't cooked like she used to. They hadn't eaten well. Their smiles that had vanished that morning did not come back. Gunen smoked hookah more than before and whenever he got anxious, he released his anxiety through smoke. He borrowed *biri* from Gafur and smoked until Gafur made him aware of the number of *biris* he'd smoked in one sitting. He'd always disliked smoking *biris* because of the smell. He enjoyed smoking hookah. Now frustration and concern conspired to induce him to smoke *biris* with as much interest as in hookah. But smoking hookah lessened his tension more than smoking *biris*.

Gunen and Gafur searched for the cow in their village. Not finding her, they planned to go to Fakir Sahib, who was a fortune teller.

*

Gunen and Gafur entered Fakir Saab's room. Gunen took a quick look at the room: a chair in front of a bench, a bed to the west of the room, three windows on the southern wall—four on the western and eastern, two on each. The windows were open.

A famous fortune teller, Fakir Saab was a tall, slim,

and straight man of fair complexion. He was between seventy and eighty. His silver-white long beard made him look pious, like a saintly person, and enhanced the dignity of his personality. After sitting in the chairs side by side, Gunen told him about the cow and humbly asked him to tell them where she was and if they'd be able to find her.

Raising his right hand like in a blessing, Fakir Saab closed his eyes and started saying rosary in a meditative mood. After about ten minutes, he opened his eyes. 'The cow is being shifted from one place to another since when she's been stolen. You'll find her if you carry on searching.' Fakir Saab went to the next room, gesturing for them to keep sitting.

Gunen and Gafur kept sitting silently, looking at the door.

Fakir Saab came out, sat down. 'These red threads are charmed.' He chanted something in Arabic and tied them to their right wrists. 'Now you can search for the cow at night and remain protected, even going to the haunted places. Pay me five hundred takas after finding her.' He blessed them with his hand on their heads. He led them out of the room.

As they stepped into the beginning of the shortcut, he waved at them. Gunen saw him go in after they took the path to their village.

*

Gunen told Meghna about the prophecy and advised her to happily cook for the family and do the domestic chores like before, wearing that captivating smile he'd missed for six days. But he'd seen a shade of doubt in her eyes when she'd silently listened to him. He glanced at his right wrist she'd overlooked. 'Doubting the prophecy will be our stupidity, Meghna.'

'I don't doubt it. You must bring the cow home anyhow,' she said, her eyes into his.

*

It was a foggy and moonless evening. Meghna was cooking *moog* lentil. Gunen and Ginu were sitting on a flat wooden stool, called *piri*, their hands spread towards the woven fire.

Appon suddenly started barking. Gunen came out. Appon jumped down the veranda, ran to the backyard, and went on barking. He followed Appon, stood under the pomelo tree. Two people in black clothes passed through the turmeric field towards the rows of jackfruit trees. Leaving Appon barking, he charged into his room, took his dagger from under the mattress, and returned to where he'd stood under the tree. He couldn't watch the area the way he wanted to. The visibility was impaired. He cocked his ears and heard only insect noises. The cold breeze kissing his face, he kept standing. Appon went on barking, looking in that direction. The persons walked from behind the mango trees to the front yard and vanished into the fog. Appon stopped barking. He returned to the kitchen.

Meghna wanted to know why Appon had barked. Gunen shrugged and told her that it was just his habit. He didn't want to give her fear.

*

Meghna woke up at midnight, sweating and panting. She kicked the quilt off her body and started crying. Gunen sat up, wiped her eyes. The Decemberish cold took time to dry her sweat. In her dream, she'd seen a python crawl into their house through the window and swallow up Ginu before winding its body around him, Gunen fighting it with his dagger so it couldn't crush Ginu. He fondled her head and tried to convince her that she'd dreamed about that because of her fear, which she must remove from her mind for the health of the baby in her womb. Then, transferring Ginu to her left side, he lay down, tucked the quilt up to their chins, protectively gathered her to his chest, and shut his eyes. She started snoring. He brought Ginu between them. He lay on his left, tucked his left hand under the pillow and right one under the cheek, and closed his eyes, Ginu's head touching his back. He opened his eyes and raised his head when he heard jackals yell and dogs bark. Then, when he heard Appon bark, he made sure Appon was alert and jackals wouldn't be able to trespass on their compound and hunt ducks, which were now maybe asleep in the wooden duck canopy to the south of the granary. Jackals often entered the village to hunt chickens or ducks. He settled his head back on the pillow.

'A jackal's yelling ushers in a good omen, purifies the atmosphere,' Gunen's mother had said whenever she had heard jackals' yell.

Gunen fell asleep.

4

Being energized and inspired by the red threads and the prophecy, Gunen and Gafur searched for the cow at night miscreants of their village and other villages in its radius preferred to take advantage of. In Gunen's hand was his dagger; in Gafur's, his *ramdao*. The path they took wasn't visible beyond a few feet ahead because of the foggy atmosphere dim moonlight had added eeriness to. Their lungis, which had been folded above their knees, didn't get wet with the dew on the grass and small plants alongside the paths. Because of the gentle breeze, they felt cold despite having mufflers and shawls on. They didn't stop and talk. But, as Gunen saw Appon appear out of the fog, he made sure he'd secretly followed them and stopped to let him sniff at his legs first and then habitually rub his muzzle against them. Not sure whether they'd walked a mile or so, they resumed walking along another narrow path.

*

Appon behind them, they stopped under the one-hundred-year-old over-foliaged tree on the side of the grazing field on the bank of the little river around two hundred metres from the tree. Gunen turned his head towards Gafur scrutinizing the sea of fog as though to find something in it. The river, which flew like a spring except in the rains, had some deep areas on its bed and near the banks. The deep areas were covered with varieties of aquatic plants, including hyacinth clusters. Fish abounded in those deep areas. Gunen and Gafur, along with other villagers, had come to catch fish in the river many times. The people, who looked up at the tree with fear, refrained from fishing the ponds close to the tree, and the people, who fished those ponds, got more fish than others. In winter, their cows grazed in that grazing field too. As they stood under the tree dew drops were falling from, a gentle wind that blew from across the river stroked their faces. Under the tree, it wasn't as cold as away from under. Gunen looked up. The foliage density had blocked the view of the moon and the stars. Nothing stirred in the tree that was in slumber like the entire area was in. What had they come here for? For wasting their time under the tree? Hadn't they come here to inspect the small village on the other side of the grazing field? Most of the people of that village were professional thieves and pickpockets. They'd stopped under the tree out of curiosity. At night, they had never come to the grazing field, let alone standing under the tree to see how it looked like and to know if people feared the tree for some reason or not. The thieves often took shelter of darkness under the tree or hid stolen things, even cows and goats, as they smelled the danger of being caught.

When they turned to start walking towards the small village and heard something stir under the tree, they looked back and saw silhouettes of two people appear from down the bank. Appon barked, agitating the atmosphere. Were they the thieves who had stolen the cow? Had they watched them from down the bank? Gunen sliced the fog with his dagger and saw Gafur holding the *ramdao* towards them as if he wouldn't wait a split second to attack them, if attacked. The silhouettes vanished. Now there were no noises except the dew drops puncturing the silence. Suddenly a night bird flew off the tree. They waited but heard no more sounds and saw nothing in the tree or under. Failing to summon up the courage to go down the bank and search for the persons since they didn't know if there were more than two or if they were armed with firearms the sophisticated thieves and robbers used, they decided not to go to the thieves' village they had come out to go to.

They returned home.

5

Next night, Gunen and Gafur started for the cottage on the mound overlooking the deep pond. Careful with every step and their mouths shut, they walked through the middle of the wide path. Gafur led Gunen. He hit the path at regular intervals, with the handle of his spear. Like the previous night, he'd preferred his *ramdao* to his spear.

While silently walking, Gunen remembered the story of the deep pond and Pond Fakir; the story had passed from mouth to mouth at Munsiganj and in the surrounding villages.

In the deep pond lived two jinns in a huge iron chest. The deep pond had been made by flood waters by breaking the road the British government had failed to build though they'd tried four times. The pond was so deep none could fathom its depth even in March or April when most of the little rivers and small marshes went dry. Noises resembling faint thunders agitated the quiet around the pond and the water sprouting from upon the chest created small waves on all sides of the pond when two big snakes with tufts of hair on their heads pulled the chest out of water, after being commanded by Pond Fakir, who had also a jinn at his command to protect him in case those two jinns turned belligerent. The chest was pulled out on a new moon night. Some daring fishermen caught fishes in the pond, with hooks. People said they were ancient fishes, and they refused to eat those fishes if they were offered because they believed that eating those fishes would make them suffer from stomach ailments or the jinns would possess them and later drag them into the pond. The cunning fishermen never disclosed where they'd caught those big fishes. They were either *boal* (Wallago Fish) or *chital* (knifefish or featherback). Old Pond Fakir, who practised black magic with the help his jinn, lived in the cottage on the mound. With the help of his jinn, on a new moon night, he ritually commanded those two jinns to get him gold coins or ornaments from the chest. So in one new moon night, he blundered in commanding those two jinns in absence of his jinn. When those two jinns saw his jinn was absent, they roared with violent gestures and lifted him by the neck and disappeared into the chest. People said Pond Fakir himself was responsible for the pathetic end of his life.

On seeing the cottage standing amid fog, they stopped, became alert, and monitored the solitary area before stepping into its compound: it was a forlorn and broken cottage; it'd been built on the mound to protect it from flood waters; it was sometimes used by bold robbers or thieves as a safe hideout. They climbed up the mound, stood in front of the broken door, peeped in, and saw nothing precious but a bed and some pieces of decrepit furniture; the bed, which looked as though it'd been made years ago, was close to the wall having a small window, which, Gunen thought, would look out the pond when it was opened. Pond Fakir maybe used to take a view of the pond through that window. That the daring thieves or robbers used to take shelter in the cottage or hide the things they stole or robbed was far from the possibility they'd thought of based on gossip. Realizing there was no hope of finding the cow in the cottage or tethered to any small plants or posts around, they descended the steps, occupied by grass and creepers, and stood at the intersection of two paths before staring through the fog towards the pond. They surveyed the entire area; the dim moonlight had added an extra mystery to it. Then, as they walked ahead and stood on the broken railroad, they heard a fish break the water, looked down, and saw nothing but a deep area engulfed in fog.

They turned and walked back home.

6

On the first January morning, Gunen went to Nani's house to discuss his problem and seek her advice. She was an inspiring lady and knew a lot of things. He called her Nani. Her name was Sahera Banu.

After hearing from him about the cow, Nani first looked up at the sky and then towards the football field, where Gypsies had set up Mina Bazaar. 'I think you'd better go to Old Gypsy.'

'I never visited a gypsy camp.'

'Do you also dislike the gypsies?'

'They do acrobatics, show magic, and play with snakes.'

'The beauty I boast of even in my old age is because of them. And because of their *singa* and medicines, I can walk and move freely. A week ago, a gypsy woman applied *singa* to my waist. I went to Mina Bazaar two times to buy herbal medicine from Old Gypsy. My cheeks are not broken. Age has failed to squiggle on my face. My hair hasn't greyed.' She laughed out loud, and her laugh diminished into a lingering smile across her lips like a young woman's.

'I'm around eighty years. A mother of six sons and six daughters.' She looked at her grandchildren playing a few metres away from where they were sitting.

'You look like a fifty-year-old woman, Nani.'

She raised her right hand towards the sky. 'Allah bless Old Gypsy.'

'But Nana looks very old.'

'He doesn't use gypsy medicines. He even criticizes Old Gypsy. He can't understand his importance.' She wiped her lips on the end of her sari. 'Old Gypsy tells fortune too. He makes correct prophecies.' She glanced at the amulet on her left upper arm. 'He gave me this amulet. You can also get one from him. It'll make you powerful and courageous.' She licked her lips. 'Meet him as soon as possible. They may wind up business within two or three days and once they leave the field, it'll be difficult to find them. They don't stay at a place long.' She adjusted her veil's hood. 'They come from nowhere to vanish nowhere. They travel by boat. Boats are their houses. Their boats at anchor at the same place at the same time make a floating village.'

He got up, grabbed her hands, and touched them to his forehead.

'Riot has broken out in some parts of the country, Gunen.'

'It won't affect us.'

'Allah bless us all.'

He left.

7

Gunen entered Old Gypsy's tent after two men had come out. They'd sat on the flat wooden stools. The small room was stuffed with overused books, vials, and bottles, including dry roots of plants and their small twigs giving out acrid smells. It seemed to be his library cum lab. Interested to know how he stood those smells and if there were snakes in his room, Gunen kept staring at him arranging the books on the table in the corner of the room and caressing his long grey beard time and again. He coughed a few times and from a small box, put something into his mouth. As he slowly chewed it, Gunen noticed rhythmic movements of his mouth and beard. Did he use his medicines to keep his lips smooth and shiny? Because of his beard that was neat and clean, Gunen couldn't know if he was hollow-cheeked, but he could assume from the look of his powerful eyes that he was a powerful man. His grey brows indicated his age. He walked with a slight stoop. On his back was a burden of years. On his head was the burden of wisdom he'd gathered from his studies and experiences. But Gunen couldn't understand why he ignored his presence, whether he did so on purpose or out of habit. Then, before sitting on his stool, cross-legged—his stool was large and smooth; it was about a foot high—he turned and scowled at Gunen, combing his beard with his fingers.

'I've come to you with a purpose,' Gunen said in a soft voice, his spliced hand at his chest.

'Why did you remain silent?'

'You didn't speak.' Gunen scratched the tip of his nose. 'May I call you Nana?'

Old Gypsy nodded, a glowing smile cracking through his lips.

'Are these your books, Nana?'

'They belonged to my ancestors. Now they belong to me.'

'How can you stand the smells?'

Old Gypsy smiled, smoothed his beard. 'I enjoy the smells.'

Gunen introduced himself, told him about the cow.

'You'll find the cow if you search with confidence. Confidence is a person's rocket booster. Confidence is above prophecy. Confidence triggers a person's dormant power and courage,' Old Gypsy said while twisting the cowlicks on his left brow.

'Can you change people's destiny, Nana?'

'Your karma builds your destiny. If I can't change my destiny myself, how can I change people's destiny?' Old Gypsy cleared his throat. 'We're snake charmers. We catch snakes and play with them in front of people to collect money. We sell herbal medicines and cure people of strange ailments. We help the mainstream people. But ...'

'Go on, Nana.'

'But the mainstream people don't trust us. They think us uncivilized. They don't associate with us. They keep us detached from their society. So we live in our society, and they live in theirs.'

'Why are you a gypsy?'

'Because my ancestors were gypsies. Because moving from one place to another is our heredity, our culture. Because ... because ...'

'Don't you trust the mainstream people?'

'No.'

'Why?'

'Do you have time to listen to a story?'

Gunen nodded and shifted for comfort.

'Some gypsies live in boats. So they're called boat people. Some gypsies catch snakes for a living. They're called snake charmers.' Old Gypsy caressed his beard with his fingers. 'We're also boat people. Some of us are snake charmers.'

'Is it your story?'

'Will you listen to the story of Merina and Mohir?'

'Yes, I will.'

'Mohir was the only son of a rich man. He was an M A student. He was healthy and handsome. People admired his kind-heartedness. Merina was a gypsy girl. She lived with her grandmother and uncle. She called her grandmother Nani and her uncle Chacha. They loved her most and taught her everything they knew. She could catch the most ferocious cobra alone. The snakes danced the best dances to the tune of her flute. Her enticing beauty, charm, good figure, fair complexion, courage, strength, and expertise made her famous among the gypsies of other boat villages too. She was a luscious young girl. She was soft-hearted. She was always full of smiles. She never wiped her smile off her face. Not only the gypsy guys, but also the guys of mainstream society vied with one another to win her over. But she didn't look at any guys. She never went alone to the villages. She knew people leered at her. She was committed to her profession and helped people the way she could. She was the full moon in the gypsy sky. She was their pride.'

'So interesting, Nana.'

'This is just the beginning of the story.' Old Gypsy lifted the lid of the small box and tossed something into his mouth. 'Mohir came home from Dhaka to meet his parents and friends. Whenever he would come home, he would visit his friends and the people of the village. This time he was out of luck. One afternoon, he was walking through his village with one of his friends. They were so absorbed in the talk that they didn't notice a snake just in front of their feet. His friend saw the snake first. Just when he pulled Mohir back, the snake bit Mohir's toe and slithered down the grassy path. It was a black cobra with yellow horizontal stripes on its body. It was around twelve feet long. Mohir immediately fell to the ground and became senseless. With the help of some people, his friend carried him home. His parents broke down. The entire village gathered in their compound. An *ojha* was called in to neutralize the venom by chanting mantras. He couldn't succeed. Some more *ojhas* were called in. None could do anything. Mohir's parents became hopeless. All the people who were there became hopeless. Then, following the advice of the chief *ojha*, a raft was made with banana trunks and Mohir was laid on it under a mosquito net. His father gave twenty-five thousand takas and a letter in an envelope with Mohir. In the letter he wrote that those who would be able to save the victim would deserve to take the money. With a pair of stakes, a hurricane lamp was fixed to a trunk of the raft so at night it could attract attention. The raft, later floated in a river, went downstream. The venom needed to be neutralized within seven days. After seven days none would be able to save his life. The details were in the letter.'

Not dropping his eyelids, Gunen took a deep breath and gulped.

Old Gypsy again tossed something into his mouth and looked at Gunen, a dry smile flickering across his lips. 'It was evening. Merina and her Nani were cooking in their boat. Merina's Chacha was relaxing in a chair on the bow. In the other boats, other gypsies were busy the way they used to be. Merina was a good cook too. She'd learned cuisine from her Nani.'

'Who cooks for you?'

'Don't interrupt.' Old Gypsy looked at Gunen over the thick rims of his spectacles. 'Merina first saw the light. She became curious to see what it was. She influenced her Nani and Chacha to row the boat down to where the light was. As they went there, they saw a person lying covered with a bedspread, under a mosquito net on a raft close to the bank. Merina leaned down to the raft and removed the bedspread. A handsome young man was lying on the raft. She guessed what had happened to him. She felt his pulse. Her heart melted away. She urged Nani and Chacha through her tears to help her carry him from the raft onto the bank. After he'd been brought to the bank, Merina read the letter. "The venom must be neutralized before dusk tomorrow. The time is very short," Merina said to Nani and Chacha.'

'Don't stop, Nana.'

'Nani chanted her mantras during the night. She couldn't succeed. Chacha couldn't succeed either. Some other gypsies from other boats also came to help them. Night rolled to morning. Morning rolled to noon. Except Merina, all of them gave up hope. To help Merina, Nani made the last attempt. That was the most dangerous attempt. She found an earthen pot covered with a red piece of cloth and put a fistful of earth in it before chanting her mantras. After a few minutes, she heard loud hissing noises. She got frightened. She flinched away from the pot. She couldn't move. Her hands went limp. Her mouth dropped open. Her chest heaving, Merina crouched behind Nani. Sure, the snake was alive, Merina became hopeful. "Don't give up, Nani. Don't give up." "If the snake is brought here, anything may happen to anyone. And it'll first attack me. You can't save me from its attack. I'll give you twenty-five thousand takas. Don't take it as a challenge. You can never save him. The venom has entered his muscle cells. The snake is very venomous. I cured many snake-bitten people. But he's different. Now his whole body is venom. Don't take the risk of your life and spoil your energy and labour." "Nani, I'm not greedy for money. I don't want to save him for money. I feel it's my duty to save him. So I must save him. For him I can take the risk of my life. I can give my life for him." "Look at the slanting sun, Merina. When I fail, you can never succeed." "You never discouraged me like this, Nani. I won't give up. Just bless me with the power of your hands. I've decided to give my life to him. I must save him. I'll give him my longevity. I must see him sit up and smile. If you don't force the snake to come suck the venom, I'll suck it myself and gulp it down." "Then you want me to send the cowries?" Nani asked, looking into Merina's tearful eyes. "Yes. I'll face the snake. I'll face its ferocity," Merina said. "Who'll buy forty *sers* of milk and a white goat? I don't have enough money in my purse," Nani said. Merina immediately took her earrings off her ears and passed them to Chacha to buy milk and goat. Nani took out three cowries and sent them in three directions by empowering them with the magic of her mantras so they could force the snake to come suck the venom from Mohir's toe, though she was aware of what might happen if she failed to subdue its venomous anger. Now Merina became desperate and sought Nani's permission to apply the mantras herself. Though reluctant, Nani finally permitted her.' Old Gypsy stood up, opened the window shut by the blowing wind, and came back to his seat.

'Then what happened, Nana?'

'Then on Nani's instructions, a large pan was filled with forty *sers* of cow milk. Then the pan and a white goat were placed near Mohir's head. And Merina took off her clothes and got into the river with the pot covered with a red piece of cloth. She stood in naval-deep water and invoked the snake by chanting her special mantras even Nani couldn't dare to chant. She went on chanting the mantras nonstop. Around a hundred people stood behind her on the bank. She was fixedly watching the water ahead of her. Nani was wailing. She knew the invoked snake would become almost mad with anger in such a situation.

She wasn't sure if Merina would be able to control the snake when it came up with the violent demonstration of its fury. She also said her prayers for Merina's safety.' Nana wiped the corners of his mouth and took a deep breath.

'Did the snake come up before dusk?'

'The sun was leaning towards the horizon. There was little time in hand. Not a single person left the bank. They were anxiously waiting for the last dramatic moment. Merina didn't look at the sun. She kept on chanting her mantras. Now her voice wasn't as strong as her voice used to be. She hadn't drunk even a drop of water since she'd seen Mohir. Despite her weakness, she didn't stop chanting the mantras. Then, all of a sudden, the water ahead of her started heaving as though some powerful creature was moving under. It appeared the water was boiling. The snake was coming up, churning the water with its force and fury. It was that snake. It climbed up the bank with desperate urgency, sending a spell of stillness all about. It slithered up to Mohir's toe it'd bitten. It sucked the venom and poured it into the pan of milk, making the milk turn bluish black. Then it hungrily bit the throat of the white goat after winding its entire body around him. It left him when he fell to the ground and succumbed to its venom. It hurried into the river and vanished. Merina had then been on her bent knees near Mohir. She'd watched and commanded the snake, throwing dust towards it while chanting mantras. Merina stood up, took her clothes from Nani's hand, and put them on. Nani sat beside Mohir's head, smoothed his hair, and then slapped his scalp three times. Merina anxiously looked at the sun that was about to meet the horizon. She hunkered down close to Mohir. She took his pulse and felt it beat. A smile radiated along her face. Her tiredness vanished in an instant. She looked as vibrant and vigorous as before. Then Merina and Nani began to nurse Mohir. Merina massaged his feet and Nani smeared his head with herbal oil. Mohir opened his eyes and saw Merina hovering over his face and said, "Who are you? Where am I?" "I'm Merina. Don't worry. You're in a safe place," she said, taking his head in her lap.' Old Gypsy looked out the window, caressing his beard.

'Don't stop.'

'Then they carried him to their boat. Merina fed him milk-soaked rice with her fingers. She told him the story of what had happened to him and how he'd been saved. He took off his gold ring and put it on her left ring finger. He accepted her as his wife. He made the full moon and the stars his witnesses. He made a solemn promise to the moon and the stars that he'd never leave her in any circumstances. Then he went to sleep with his head in her lap. She remained awake all night to take care of him.' Nana closed his eyes as though in a meditative mood, took a long breath, and then licked his lips.

'Have you finished telling the story?'

'Keep listening. Now you'll know why gypsies don't trust the mainstream people.'

Gunen stretched and scratched his upper lip.

'Nani understood what had happened between Mohir and Merina. "This relationship isn't possible, Mohir. Your society will thrust her back to her boat village," Nani said. "I love her. I can't live without her. She has already become the part of my life," Mohir said, a tone of determination in his soft voice. Then a messenger was sent to Mohir's father with details in a letter. His parents came with their people on a boat. They became so happy about seeing their son. As a reward, he offered more than twenty-five thousand takas to Merina and Nani. The offer was refused. Mohir's parents came to know about the relationship. They got angry. They made an offer of more money. "I didn't take the risk of my life for money," Merina said after refusing the second offer. Merina was as adamant as Mohir. The situation took a new turn. So unable to convince the lovers to leave each other, Mohir's father agreed in front of the people who were there and especially the gypsies, that they'd go back home with Merina and marry his son to her in their village. His father, failing to convince his son while going upstream towards their village, executed his plan he'd secretly made with his people. He tied Mohir's hands and feet and asked Merina to change her decision that would cost her dear. That was his warning. "I can jump into the river, but I can't change my decision. I can't live without my Mohir," Merina said, her voice plaintive. Then his father ordered his men to tie her hands and feet too. After they carried out his order, he asked her again to change her decision. But she was adamant. Mohir was squirming to free his hands and feet. Failing to untie her hands and feet, she, Merina, cried for help. Her cries caused the water of the river to roll into ripples. The boat swayed. Mohir sought his mother's help, though he knew she supported his father. None listened to them. "Throw her into the river," his father ordered. They obeyed. Mohir fainted. Going home, his father brought the best doctor for his son's medical treatment. But his son didn't recover from the shock. He went mad. Whenever he remembered her, he went to that place and spent time, sitting on the riverbank, thinking that she'd rise from the water with her shining smile and embrace him into her supple bosom in the succulent light of the sun.' Old Gypsy fingered his beard.

Gunen remained silent for a while. What was he there for? Though the story burdened his mind with sorrow, he decided to take the amulet and leave for his home as soon as possible. 'The person who wears your charmed amulet, remains protected. The amulet gives them power, strength, courage, and victory.'

'Who told you about the amulet?'

Gunen told him about his Nani, whom Old Gypsy identified from the details of her physical description.

Old Gypsy laughed a brittle laugh. 'I'll give you an amulet for free if you agree to pass a box to Jahangir Alam at Monpara.'

'Monpara is about six miles from here. And I don't know Jahangir Alam.'

'He's known to many people in that locality. It won't be a problem.' Old Gypsy stood up and looked out the window before going to open the drawer of his table in the far corner of the room. He took out a slip of paper, adjusted his spectacles, and while reading it, he glanced at Gunen twice and nodded his head. He smiled his special smile and passed it to Gunen, commanding with his brows to unfold it right away.

Gunen unfolded it. 'I'm illiterate.'

'Show the slip of paper to someone if you forget the name and address.'

'Riot has broken out against the Hindus in some parts of the country. I'm a Hindu.'

'My amulet will protect you. Decide if you can do it for me. Jahangir can help you find your cow.'

The cow crossed Gunen's mind. She was like a member of their family. In hard days, she helped them with her milk Ginu also depended on. Gunen swallowed hard and touched his forehead. Despite the January wind through the window into the room, he felt like taking off his sweater. He had no alternative but to accept the condition as Old Gypsy adamantly declined to sell him an amulet.

Old Gypsy took an amulet from his wooden box on his cot and stood close to Gunen, the amulet in the cup of his right palm. It was rectangular in shape. It had two rings attached to its sides, and a twisted red skein was threaded through the rings and tied tight so it didn't slip off the hold of the skein.

'I understand you promise you'll pass the box to Jahangir.'

'Yes. I promise.'

Gunen didn't put importance to the promise. He wasn't so stupid that he'd go to Monpara and take the risk of his life. Old Gypsy couldn't understand that he'd agreed to carry out his order just to be empowered by the magical amulet he needed most to boldly search for the cow and find her to bring happiness to the family. Meghna had expected to give the cow's milk to the baby to be born in January when the cow would also calve. He decided to open the box and throw it into the marsh he'd go by.

While chanting mantras, Old Gypsy tied the amulet to Gunen's right upper arm, with the red skein. 'Now promise again by touching the amulet on your arm. If you break your promise, the amulet will work against you and the power I give you will vanish.'

'I promise by touching the amulet on my arm that I'll deliver the box to Jahangir Alam.'

Old Gypsy patted Gunen's head. 'Don't fear anything or anyone. None can harm you if the amulet is on your arm. Take care it always remains on your arm. Never be afraid to fight for the truth and justice. Always think and act positively. Okay?'

'Okay.'

Old Gypsy handed Gunen the box wrapped in coarse hide of some animal and asked him to start his journey next day early in the morning so he could return home in the afternoon. Gunen glanced at the amulet on his arm and politely received the box.

'For the first time, I've seen a trust-worthy man. You're so intelligent. So innocent. People can depend on you. You'll never be defeated in life. Keep the amulet on your arm forever. Always tie it with a red skein when this skein wears out,' Old Gypsy said. 'Jahangir is a powerful man. I'm sure you'll find your cow with his help.'

They waved good-bye.

Then, while going past the marsh under the thin fog melted by the sun, he glanced at the box and then at the marsh on his right. Before throwing it away, he must secretly open the box in his room and see its contents.

8

Gunen opened the box, sitting on the bed. It was stuffed with hundred-taka denomination. He took out the amulet. He counted out the money: one lakh and twelve thousand. How had the money come to Old Gypsy? Were Old Gypsy and Jahangir Alam linked to each other? There was maybe something behind this money. There was maybe something wrong somewhere. He first put the amulet in the box, and then he put the money on the amulet, like Old Gypsy had put them. Then, placing it in his trunk, he locked it and hid the key under the mattress.

Was Jahangir Alam a good man or a bad man?

Suddenly, he changed his mind and, dismissing his promise he'd made to Old Gypsy, decided to embezzle the money that would give him power and confidence and enable him to live happily with his family, like a rich man, without labouring hard in the corn fields. But the moment he looked at his amulet and remembered the cow, he felt his greed fade away and determined to deliver the box to Jahangir Alam, following Old Gypsy's instructions.

Before starting for Monpara, he sent his wife and son to his maternal uncle's at Pipradanga.

9

Gunen felt unable to move when he saw the field he was going past lying like a deserted place blanketed by the early morning fog. Where had the gypsies gone? Had they ended their business because of the rioting? The gypsies normally don't wind up their business before a month. He walked into the field littered with the things they'd used and left.

Then, going up to where Old Gypsy had built his tent, he sat on the trampled-on grass amid the mixed smells of medicines and oil still faintly rising from the ground. The grass under the table Old Gypsy had put his books and medicines on had turned pale. Not twitching his nose like before, he closed his eyes, deeply breathed in the smells, and tried to hear if Old Gypsy's voice echo all about. Too puzzled to decide about whether he should break his promise, he looked at the amulet and kept looking at it, and when he failed to gather the courage that he needed most to start the journey, he mentally abased himself for agreeing to accept the burden of responsibility. He straightened his head, forced the feeling of fear and risk of life out of his mind, and resolved to put the money in Jahangir Alam's hand so he could ask for his help to find the cow.

He stood up and started walking towards Monpara, with a mental note to return home before dusk fell.

*

After about two miles, Gunen arrived at the meeting point of two paths. Confused about the path he should take for Monpara, he waited for the man speed-walking from the direction of the marsh glittering in the sun. The fog had started to thin out.

Within a few minutes, the man came up, a fish net on his shoulder and a creel in his right hand and his legs below his knees spattered with mud. When Gunen wanted to know from him about the exact location of Monpara, he said that it was four miles from where they were. His eyes flitted between Gunen's look and the bag clutched to his chest. He introduced himself as Mubarak Ali and told Gunen to walk back and take the shortcut across the Python Bridge; unless he crossed the Python Bridge, he must cross another bridge over a river.

'What are you carrying in the bag?' Mubarak asked.

'I can't tell you about it,' Gunen answered, his stare piercing Mubarak's eyes.

'Why?'

'You'll throw me away into the marsh if I tell you what there is in my bag.'

'Are you carrying some valuable things?'

With his timid eyes, Gunen measured the intensity of Mubarak's curiosity. 'There is a box in the bag. It belongs to Old Gypsy. Do you know Old Gypsy?'

'He's a snake charmer. He practises black magic. I never go to him. I never buy medicines from gypsies. Open the bag. I want to see its content.'

Gunen placed the bag in front of him. 'Open the box yourself. I can't take the risk of my life.'

'What's in the box?' Mubarak didn't lift his focus from it.

'A small king cobra.'

Mubarak stood up, stepped back. 'What are you thinking of?'

'I'm thinking of passing the box to you. Old Gypsy instructed me only to pass it to a strong and courageous man and to never throw it anywhere.' Gunen moistened his dry lips with the tip of his tongue. 'The snake is sleeping in the box. It'll sleep until tomorrow night. If I throw the box away, the snake will wake up. It'll break the box open and come out. Old Gypsy raised it with magical power. It can fly too. It never forgets its enemies. Don't make me its enemy, Mubarak-bhai. I don't want you to be its enemy either. You can never get rid of the cobra by throwing the box into the marsh. If you don't believe me, you may try to know if I'm telling the truth. Before you throw it away, I hope you'll kindly give me a chance to kneel and pray for its mercy. But I'll never ask you to throw it away. You can only take it home and pass it to a gypsy if you want to.'

Throwing a scowl at Gunen's face, when Mubarak turned to follow his path, Gunen started walking, and he didn't stop until he got to the bank of the marsh, after about ten to twelve minutes. Gunen walked down the road and sat on his heels where it slanted to the hyacinth clusters at the water's edge and urinated. He looked down at the path squirming along the bank of the marsh towards the Python Bridge. Reluctant to cross the bridge for a shortcut, he stepped down the road and took the path in the opposite direction of the bridge.

He walked for about thirty minutes before finding himself on a dusty, wide path having the prints of cows' hooves in the dust he kicked and saw there was no wind stream to carry the dust. The path rose to a dirt road. He hit the road, stood in its middle, and tried to see if there were any men, then, after walking for some time, he saw a group of men and stopped to let them come up: they weren't rioters; they didn't have weapons in their hands; they were with beards; they looked pious—pious people are truthful and generous, and generous people are harmless.

Gunen introduced himself as Amin Alfarukh from Munsiganj, and then as he told them he was going to his cousin Jahangir Alam's, he noticed the face of the man, who had struck up the conversation of queries, drop open. They went to a side, talked about something, and thoughtfully looked at his face; the shades of sympathy in their eyes lessened his fear a bit.

'Your cousin is a notorious robber. He's a terror in the surrounding villages. Do you know it?' a man said.
'Riot has broken out in the villages. Now your cousin is also maybe rioting. You should go back home.'

'What's the cause for the riot?'

'Kafirs have stolen our Prophet's Holy Hair from Hazrat Baal Mosque in Kashmir.'

'I'm not afraid of rioters. The Hindus are targets.'

Gunen looked at the minaret of the mosque he could clearly see from there. 'Are you going to the mosque to say Friday prayer?'

'Yes.'

Saying *'asalamualaikum'* to them, Gunen resumed walking, remembering Old Gypsy's direction. He walked fast because he'd seen a *musulli* pay attention to his bag. He looked back and when he didn't see them, he thought they'd gone to the mosque. He was going east. The sun said. Now he made sure the money was not Jahangir Alam's honest earnings and decided to return home, not taking the risk of his life. But he couldn't do so. He felt wedged between promise and risk; it was very unsafe to walk through the riot-torn villages; confused in the extreme, he plopped himself down on the road and kept sitting until he heard human noises, which got him to get up and walk faster than before so he could cross the bridge over the river and take the road to Jahangir Alam's. Aware that he didn't have even a second to waste on the riverbank, he crossed the bridge and walked on ahead, terrified as though being chased. As he came under a leafy tree he couldn't identify, he stopped, huffing and puffing. The noises were coming towards him. For immediate safety, he climbed up the tree. The view widened out and the bridge became clearly visible. He felt fear tighten on his nerves and render him unable to move when he saw the people running helter-skelter to save themselves, to save their children clinging to them being chased by armed men; the women trying and failing to run like the men while keeping their children from falling and controlling their clothes; all of them, men, women, and children, crying for help and mercy. The young girls and women, who looked behind repeatedly, looked more panicked. There were a few beautiful young girls.

He didn't know where they were going, but he could guess they were running to find a safe shelter. The villages were burning. With his trembling fingers, he felt the box and the dagger in his bag. He swallowed hard. He checked his sneeze midway. He remembered his family and relatives, the Hindu families in their village and in the villages around, and worried about riot he didn't know if it had spread in those villages too and became concerned about their safety. The box suddenly felt so heavy. What should he do? Should he throw it away towards the river from where he was in the tree and get down to follow the people on the run?

He changed his mind when he saw swords, spears, daggers, big machetes, and lathis in the hands of the people chasing the men and women—they'd picked up whatever they'd found to pick up to use as weapons. Some rioters shouted their special slogans; some abused the Hindus, using obscene language; some came from opposite direction, creating pressures from both ends. The victims had no ability to move from the middle of the bridge. Unable to face the rioters from both ends, the men, and women along with their children jumped off the bridge into the river; some couldn't find time to jump off; some didn't jump off because the children were clutching on to them; but some women jumped into the river with their children. The frenzy of attack became so intense that nothing could be heard except the anomalous noises of the victims and the rioters. Some rioters picked some young girls and women and threw their children on the road to be trampled on and escaped into whatever direction they thought better. They dragged the women and the girls along the road. They kicked them. They slapped them hard on their faces as they cried aloud.

Afraid of the rioting, Gunen, who couldn't dare to get down, breathed hard and shut his eyes, not sure if he'd be able to climb down the tree until it was evening, and then as he opened his eyes, he saw those people still on the bridge and got too frightened to go to Jahangir Alam's through the riot-torn areas, taking the risk of his life.

*

When the rioters were gone, Gunen climbed down the tree. Having seen the slippers and pieces of clothes, scattered here and there on the road, he stood still, and then he hunkered down, his eyes not moving away from the stains of blood on the dust and on the pale blades of grass on either side of the road. He felt sorrow for the victims. The faces of his son and wife crossed his mind and brought tears to his eyes. He regretted going to Old Gypsy and why he couldn't pluck up the courage to directly abdicate the responsibility Old Gypsy had imposed on him. He slapped his forehead, stood up, and looked towards the river the sun was glinting in. A quiet had settled in the entire area. The decision he must go back home in mind, he walked towards the bridge, but his energy seeped away as he stood at its entrance and stared at the remnants of cruelties: the men on women; the women on men; the children still clutching on to their parents or relatives, signs of fear in their blank eyes; blood clotting; blood on their bodies, on the planks of the bridge; some men and women, and children were chopped into parts; they seemed to have struggled hard to defend themselves before meeting with failures that had robbed them of their souls. He cast his fearful look down into the river and saw some bodies in the river too—men, women, children; some bodies floating in shallow water; a baby in a woman's arm tightly pressed against her breasts. What was the guilt of those people? He wondered. Was it their guilt that they were Hindus living in East Pakistan? Was it their guilt that their parents had lived in the country for centuries? Didn't the country belong to them? Had they caused impurity to their motherland? How could all this happen in such a short time?

He looked away from the river and the bridge, turned back, and started running like a man possessed, the bag clamped to his chest, and he somehow stopped falling on his front as he tripped over a broken brick. He sat down to recover breaths. He didn't know if he had run in the direction of their village, but when he looked back and saw the tree he'd been in, he knew his mistake had brought him in the direction of Monpara. Now that he had no courage to cross the bridge and he was too tired and weak and sick to walk the long distance back home, he dragged his feet up to the small tree on the side of the road, sat at its foot, and leaned against it's smooth trunk, his legs spread apart to get relaxed and his sorrowful look set on the grazing cattle in the fields. Though he didn't see smoke and fire in the villages beyond the fields and no people being chased, he still couldn't make sure that the rioting had abated.

Finally, feeling determined to hide the box exactly at the place, where Old Gypsy had set his table, he half-shut his eyes, summoned the energy and courage to cross the bridge strewn with the remnants of the massacre and to run the way his legs allowed so he could reach the field before it was afternoon.

*

Just arriving in the field, Gunen found a pointed splinter of wood and started digging the earth to hide the box, and then when he heard footsteps behind him, he looked back and saw a fifty-plus man with thick moustache and a deep cut mark looking deeper than it would've looked without the anxieties and fear orbiting his face; before being certain he was none but that man, he remembered Old Gypsy, who had told him about those two special marks on Jahangir Alam's face. He was maybe sitting behind the trees, Gunen thought, stood up, and demanded his introduction to become certain about his identity.

'What are you doing here? What's there in this box?' Jahangir Alam looked at the box and the small hole, the splinter was lying by.

'Do you know Old Gypsy?'

'Yes.'

'Did you leave your money with him?'

'How do you know it?'

'You didn't answer my question.'

'I'm a robber. I dropped the money in Old Gypsy's hand when I saw the police in Mina Bazaar. I came here to buy an amulet.' Jahangir Alam didn't withdraw his focus from the box.

'How much money?'

'One lakh twelve thousand.'

'This is your money. Old Gypsy asked me to pass it to you. I couldn't dare to go beyond the tree on the other side of the bridge.' Gunen handed him the box.

'What were you doing here?'

'I was digging the earth to hide the money. I thought the owner would come here or Old Gypsy would find it when he would dig the earth to set up his tent next year. I didn't want to take the money home. This is not my money.' Gunen looked up at the sun and knew from its position that it'd take at least four hours to set. 'You'll find your amulet in the box.'

'Did you open the box?'

Gunen nodded. Jahangir Alam sat down, emptied the box on the shawl he was wearing, and counted out the money. Keeping looking up at Gunen's face, he told Gunen to tell him the name of his village, and after Gunen had told him the name, he stood up and embraced Gunen before going to the trees and returning with a sword in his hand. Gunen kept staring at the sword, wondering if Jahangir Alam would attack him; but, instead of doing that, when he grasped Gunen's hand and told he'd learned from people that riot had occurred at Munsiganj as well, Gunen jerked his hand free from his grasp, lifted his bag from near the splinter, and started running towards Munsiganj, being followed by Jahangir Alam.

10

As soon as Gunen and Jahangir Alam entered the village, the wind blew smells of cinders into their noses. The rioters had caused havoc to the Hindu houses. Gunen felt a rush of panic.

By the time he stumbled into his compound, he lost his balance and fell off and remained lying until water, sprayed on his face, made him open his eyes: Jahangir Alam was sitting beside him, his hands wet and his sword near his feet. Jahangir Alam wiped his tears with the heels of his hands and helped him sit up. He looked around and saw the houses had been badly reduced to embers; the corrugated tin sheets had been looted; no signs of property in the charred remains. He worried about the cows. He worried about Appon. He began to cry. Jahangir Alam tried to console him, smoothing his head, and wiping his tears time and again.

*

Then they went to Gafur's. His house had been burned down too. A hammer pounding his heart, Gunen loudly called out to Gafur, his wife, and their eight-year-old son Hamid. He heard no voices and saw not even a creature emerge from the silence of the remains. He threw himself onto the veranda and flailed his hands, wailing for Gafur and his family, and then, like before, Jahangir Alam helped him sit up and tried to comfort him with the tenderness of his touch on his head and back. His tears had brought tears to Jahangir Alam's eyes as well.

'I can get some information from Nani. Let's go to Nani's, Alam-bhai.'

*

Nani, who came out running from inside, just seeing them, embraced Gunen so tight he felt he would've suffocated unless she released him.

'Meghna and Ginu where?' Nani asked.

'At Pipradanga.'

'There has been rioting in that village too.'

With tear-sodden eyes, Appon appeared out of the blue. His look and belly said he was starving. He stroked Gunen's legs with his tail and stood on his hind legs to lick his left elbow near his muzzle.

Nani wiped Gunen's eyes with the hem of her sari. 'The rioters looted your properties. They took your cows away. Gafur fought the rioters. They later set fire to his house too. He escaped from our village. With his son and wife. A rioter's blow on his left hand. I bandaged his hand. Gafur for the Hindus. Helped them join the exodus to India.' Nani sounded nervous.

Jahangir Alam came forward and stood close to her, his focus on her face. 'My name is Jahangir Alam.'

'You the robber? Old Gypsy told me about you.'

'Didn't he tell you anything more than that I'm a robber?'

'He trusts me with the secrets of many people of the villages. I never belie his trust.'

'Nani, now I want to take your leave,' Gunen said, his voice trembling.

'Where will you go?'

'Pipradanga.'

'It'll be evening when you'll reach Pipradanga. Rioting is going on. I advise you to stay the night at our house. You'll go there in the morning.'

'Nani is right, Gunen,' Jahangir Alam said.

Nani led them into the sitting room, gave them water to drink, and asked them to eat puffed rice or rice flake, whatever they liked, because they looked hungry. Meanwhile, Appon stood at the door of the room as if he wasn't in a mood to lose Gunen, and since he'd met Gunen, he'd kept him tied to his look saying he'd regained his hope he'd lost. He thought Appon would starve to give up his life unless he took Appon to where he moved.

*

In the morning, Nani gave Gunen rice flakes and molasses in a bundle, as provisions, before wetting his cheeks with her goodbye kisses, runnels of tears down her cheeks. She advised him to come back when the situation returned to normal and gave him assurance that her family, with Gafur's help, would rebuild the house.

Nani fondled Gunen's head like she used to fondle it when he praised her and ground her betel nut and betel leaf in her mortar. He felt grief tighten his voice and thought he'd miss her as he'd miss his motherland, where his ancestors, he couldn't help repeating, had lived for centuries, and realized how difficult it was to leave a country, though he'd often told his wife that they'd better leave the country because of Taimoor's atrocious activities. Kind Muslims outnumbered the cruel ones. Gunen couldn't meet Nana, Nani's husband, their sons, daughters-in-law, and grandchildren. They'd left the village during rioting.

'I'm protected and empowered by Old Gypsy and his amulet,' she said.

Gunen touched his amulet. 'I'm also protected and empowered by Old Gypsy and his amulet, Nani.'

'Never leave it.'

Gunen touched her feet. She again kissed him on his forehead. Wiping her tears, he gave her a goodbye kiss, Jahangir Alam watching them, his lips quivering. The end of her sari pressed against her lips and tears down her cheeks, she walked them to the path to Gunen's house and kept standing, a silhouette of a statue, until they diminished from her sight.

*

Just reaching the compound, Gunen passed the bundle to Jahangir Alam and went to the stubble field, paddy stalks raking at his legs. Cows were grazing. Birds were flying over the cows and catching insects. Though he knew he'd never find the brown cow and the other ones, he looked for them like he used to do when they'd been let loose to graze on the grass in the stubble fields. He scanned all the fields around and stored them in his memory so he could mentally tour those places when he missed the motherland.

*

In the compound, Gunen focused on every object before his eyes and filled his memory with whatever he considered his legacy. He'd live his life with those stale memories. He looked at Appon. Was Appon also trying to preserve those things in his memory? Being followed by Jahangir Alam, he stepped into his bedroom, stood amid cinders, and scrutinized the destruction: near the old trunk under the burned cot was a medium-sized glass bottle peeping out from under a half-burned splinter. He hunkered down, upturned the trunk, chased the debris away with his right hand, and lifted the bottle and saw its cork had been darkened by fire's tongue; he uncorked it, dug out a fistful of soil with the point of his dagger, and filled it with the soil. He made obeisance to the floor. Appon sniffed at the burned objects in the rooms as if trying to find something important, then he lay flat on his stomach and nuzzled the floor with his muzzle. Wiping his eyes, Gunen stood up, touched the bottle to his forehead, and put it in his bag. Appon was at his heels. He'd never behaved like that. It seemed that he doubted something.

'I'll take you with me, Appon. Don't worry.' Gunen stroked Appon's head.

'What'll you do with it?' Jahangir Alam pointed to the bottle.

'This is my legacy.'

Through the remains, Gunen pulled Jahangir Alam

into the courtyard. 'This is our bench. We used to sit on it. Fire left its only one leg. The chair is reduced to cinders.' He remembered how Taimoor had lifted the chair and dropped it. 'I'll now go to Pipradanga. To bring Meghna and Ginu.' He looked at Appon standing close to him, biting the strap of his bag. 'I'll convince my two *mamas* to accompany me and join the exodus. If we can't live here, they can't either.'

'I can't leave you alone. I'll escort you to the riverbank. Nani gave you one thousand takas.' Jahangir Alam opened the box, counted out twelve thousand takas, and forced the money into Gunen's hand. 'This money will come to your use when you'll be in extreme need for money in India. This is my address. Old Gypsy wrote it out for you. Keep it with you and write me letters whenever you find time.'

They started for Pipradanga. Appon followed them.

11

Gunen, Meghna, and Ginu, escorted by Jahangir Alam, arrived at the bank of the Brahmaputra. Not a single refugee was on the bank. There was only one boat at anchor. About fifty people of different age groups were in the boat. When a boatman leaned to where the anchor was, Gunen thought the boatman was going to weigh it and raised his hand to draw his attention to them. Jahangir Alam also waved to the boatman.

Gunen, Meghna, and Ginu touched Jahangir Alam's feet. Jahangir Alam left the sword near his feet, blessed them with his hands, and then motioned the boatman sitting at the stern to get off. When the boatman got off, Jahangir Alam took him to a side, talked to him, and put something in his hand. The boatman glanced at Gunen over and over.

Meghna and Ginu got into the boat. Gunen stood on the bank and looked about. He and Gafur had caught lobsters with their cast nets in the river. He bowed to the earth of his country he'd never be able visit in his life. He mentally bowed down to the river too. He couldn't remember how many times he'd crossed it, but he could remember crossing it in a small boat loaded with ripe jackfruits, the gunwale just about two inches above water level, Jabed Ali at the helm and his father with him crying, frozen with fear, the crying louder and louder every moment when the boat had juggled with the huge waves creating crests and troughs. It was in the rains. In the rains, the flood waters from the river offered them many fishes though their crop fields were flooded and often damaged. On boats or banana-trunk rafts, they travelled from one place to another; those memories were still alive in his mental treasure trove, which he was sure would remain forever like at present. He plucked two stalks of tall grass. The grass had weathered a pale colour. He bent them to put in his bag. He wanted to take whatever was in front of his eyes. Then, as he touched the sword, Jahangir Alam opened it, passed it to his hand, and advised him to buy a sword in India so he could fight his enemies in defence. The people in the boat made loud and incomprehensible shouts of impatience; Jahangir Alam walked Gunen down the bank and stood close to the boat the soft waves were gently stroking, making sounds as though a few dogs were noisily lapping water together. The people loudly objected to Gunen's getting into the boat, with Appon—he hadn't left him even for a while.

'Don't get into the boat along with the dog.'

'We can't allow you to take the dog with you.'

'We can't take the risk by travelling with a dog.'

'We left our dogs and cats home.'

'We shouldn't allow this man to travel with his dog.'

'It's a stray dog.'

'It's not a stray dog. It's our Appon.' Meghna stood up.

Gunen got cross. Appon moved this way and that.

'Dogs and men can't travel together in a boat.'

'That's impossible.'

'He's my friend. He doesn't bite. He'll stay with me. If he disturbs, you may throw us out of the boat.' Gunen put his right foot on the gunwale, Appon beside him.

'You're wasting our time. We must return, unloading the passengers. Riot is continuing in all parts of the country,' a boatman said. 'Rioters may attack us too.'

A pair of strong hands pulled Gunen into the boat. Before poling the boat away from the bank, a boatman struck Appon with his pole on the head so hard he flinched away from the water's edge, turning his head back to save his head from another strike. The boat took the current, but Appon didn't stop struggling to get across the river between the boat and the bank. After Jahangir Alam had prevented him from getting into the river and forced him to climb up the bank, he started running along, shaking his head from side to side, and keeping on barking though his throat had tightened; Gunen assumed Appon barked to draw his attention, to kindle the spirit of kindness in those hard-hearted people's minds; the separation tore Appon's heart apart. How could Appon live without him? Gunen stood up.

'Why do you stand up?' the boatman, who had struck Appon, said. 'Keep sitting. Don't look at the dog.'

'Appon, come on! We're in the boat, Appon! Come swim across to the boat,' Gunen shouted.

'Keep sitting, you donkey. The dog doesn't listen to you,' the boatman said.

'He's not a dog. He's our Appon.' Meghna pulled Gunen and made him sit down.

Gunen stared into the boatman's face and concluded he was an insensible man with infectious cruelty, it wasn't at all easy to stand such a man's behaviour, he wasn't a dog, he was Appon, just Appon, his friend; he was leaving the country without Appon; none could realize the situation. None could realize it because they couldn't see the cyclone in his mind. The boat's speed was diminishing Jahangir Alam into a blur that made pangs of sorrow crumple Gunen's stomach and got tears to well in his eyes. He mentally cursed the rioters he'd hate forever.

Then, suddenly, Appon waltzed into the river and started swimming to catch up with the boat steering left to take its course towards the middle. Gunen stood up, put his foot on the thwart, and motioned to jump into the river. The man, who was sitting next to him, bucketing down his advice, grasped him from behind; two other men, who joined that man, grappled him back to where he'd sat beside Meghna and Ginu crying aloud—January, the month of her expected delivery, Meghna couldn't cry as loud as Ginu. Appon struggled against the current and tried with many efforts to increase his speed to get to the boat, his head dipping and rising, and his body under water. The mid river current had slowed him down. How long would he struggle like that? Was he going to give his life for him? Compassion caught Gunen's throat.

'Go back. Go back, Appon. You can live at Gafur's

or at Nani's. They'll love you like we loved you,' Gunen shouted, splitting the heart of the river.

Gunen didn't know if Appon heard him, but he knew Appon would never change his mind, and after swimming that distance away from the bank, it was impossible for him to go back. When Appon raised his head and looked at the boat before finally diving down, Gunen began to slap his head with his hands, crying as loud as he could above the mix of the voices and the screeches the two pairs of oars chopping the river was letting out. Meghna and Ginu were also crying, staring at the river. He felt his soul had gone to join Appon's, felt weighed down by sorrow, and blamed the tragic end of Appon's life on the people aboard. They had nothing in their chests but palpitating stones. They'd called him names. They'd never called him Appon. They'd despised him as a stray dog. Reflection of cruelties was lingering in their eyes. He'd taken a dislike to them. They were not his co-travellers. They were monsters in the guises of travellers. Being hostile to Appon meant they were hostile to him. The women, except one, were not any different. All the people except a child had laughed at Appon's struggles against the river. Like they'd held Appon up to ridicule, they'd held Gunen up to ridicule too. Their minds were calloused.

Gunen remembered he'd stolen Appon from Nani's; Appon's mother had whelped two male and two female cubs; the colour of Appon's fur in bright brown had attracted him; he used to bathe Appon every day with soaps so that Appon's fur was always shiny; in the rainy season, Appon had been allowed to sleep in his room, and every winter, new warm clothes and cushioned mats had been bought for Appon. Gone were the days of his happiness. From now on, he'd have to spend his life without work animals to cultivate land. If Appon had been with him, he'd have got strength and support, like from a real friend in need. It'd have been better if he'd been able to jump into the river, and if he'd been able to jump into it, he'd have dived down, embracing his friend. Without Appon, he felt alone despite sitting beside his wife and son. Keeping looking at them for some time, he pulled the shawl up to their chins to prevent the wind from blowing cold onto their chests. He lay down so that Ginu was between him and Meghna and gathered Ginu into the warmth of his chest, not removing Meghna's left hand from upon Ginu, and despite being in closeness to the warmth of his family, he felt his mind packed with those disintegrated thoughts he didn't know when he'd be able to banish or whether he'd be able to banish them at all.

*

In the middle of the night, Meghna roused Gunen from sleep. 'The pain has become intolerable. Give me a glass of water.'

'Where will I get water?' Gunen looked about and saw some people sitting, watching the river, and some people sleeping, and he couldn't decide whom he should ask for water, because he hesitated to give her water straight from the river—his parents had taught him to be careful with drinking water and that those who drink pure water can remain free from many diseases.

Meghna sat up and started crying and asking for water aloud, her hands cupping her abdomen. When he wanted to know if there was something wrong with her, she nodded and prayed for water as though it'd make her feel comfortable.

'Why your hands on your abdomen?' Gunen bent down and touched her hands.

'The pain,' she said, her eyes begging for help.

Meanwhile, the woman, who had sympathized with Gunen all the time, came up with water in a brass glass and handed the glass to Meghna, who drank the water like she hadn't drunk water for a long time. Though he realized her thirst wasn't fully quenched, he didn't dare to ask the woman for more water, because he didn't know if she had enough water with her. Meghna returned the glass to her.

The woman sat down and scanned Meghna's face and abdomen with her eyes, and thoughtfully let out a deep sigh suggesting her diagnostic expertise in such cases. 'Is it your month?

Meghna started weeping. She looked nervous.

'It's labour pain.' The woman touched Meghna's back. 'Do you need my help?'

The reflection of love emanating from the woman's large eyes and round face brought his mother to his mind. He decided to call her *masimoni*, mother's sister. He looked at her, latent urge for her help in his eyes. She assured them of her help if they needed. She pushed her way back to her family. From where she'd sat down, she looked in their direction. He couldn't say for sure if she looked at them or at the river, which looked broader in that area.

Gunen tried to keep his eyes at the river all the time. Fog clusters adrift over the river looking silver in the straight moonlight had added eeriness to the entire atmosphere. He remembered his maternal uncles and their families. They'd told him they'd leave the country after selling their properties and meet him at the place where he'd settle. They'd taken shelter of a Muslim friend's house and felt safe though there was rioting in their village. He stretched his hands and breathed deep sighs while trying to synchronize his mind with that of the river. Does a river have a mind? He never thought of abstract things, of abstruse things. His thought level had changed since he'd seen Appon sacrifice his life for him. Nurtured by the adverse reality, his mind matured now in a strange way and made him look at the world from a strange perspective. He felt his thoughts dissolve in the river's melting silver dusted with fog particles contributing to the fog density. He had a little bit of knowledge of science that an illiterate ploughman can have by the grace of nature. With the strength of that knowledge—he never boasted of being in the know—he dissected his feelings and his views that sprouted like mushrooms in his psyche manured by the situation. He wondered if his thoughts were coherent or followed the logic. He ran his fingers through his hair. He felt the spider of insanity inching up to take over his mind and incoherently entangle it with its silk. He mentally crushed the spider and threw it away into the river.

Suddenly the old man's sniffles drew his attention. The old man was sitting with the panicked people from different backgrounds; some of them were searching for places to put their heads in; they wanted to sleep; they were also tired and anxious. Why did the old man look so morose? Was it because of the uncertain destination he was travelling to? All the people were travelling to the uncertain destination. But none of them looked so morose. How old was the old man? Maybe above seventy. Did the old man want to talk to him? He felt dispirited. He decided to sleep to control his meandering thoughts and wait for the morning when the boat was expected to hit the bank. Meghna and Ginu were sleeping, their heads on the heaps of clothes bundled into a pillow. Before lying down like before, he let his fingers gently caress her abdomen, and after lying down, he listened to the oarlocks' rhythmical screeches and the oars' chopping noises, and then the second he closed his eyes, he felt a calloused hand on his forehead and opened his eyes. The old man was squatting near his head.

Gunen sat up. 'Do you want to tell me something, Jethu?'

'Can you give me a fistful of rice flake? I haven't eaten for two days. Since the day of the rioting in our village.' Jethu rubbed his eyes.

After giving Jethu rice flake and molasses, Gunen got him a glass of water from Masimoni. He felt delight pass through his mind, like a streak of light through a crevice, when he saw Jethu let out a deep sigh and run his hand from the base of his throat down over his thoracic case and his lips part into a flicker of a smile brushing away the shades of gloominess a little.

Jethu scratched his stubbly chin and looked at the fog over the river. 'I'm separated from my family. I have become a lonely beggar. They snatched everything that I had. That I'd boasted of.'

'Couldn't you fight the rioters?'

'They attacked our village at wee hours. My wife and I were sleeping in our room. She woke me up, hearing noises. I sat up. I got confused. My two young daughters slept in the adjacent house. We called out to them. They didn't reply. We went out. The rioters were looting our properties.

We didn't see our daughters anywhere. We got anxious. A man dragged my wife to a side. I fought them to free her. They beat me for the key to the chest. I gave them the key. But they didn't stop beating me. I became senseless. When I regained senses, I saw there was no one around. I shouted for my wife. For my daughters. They didn't respond. How would they respond when they weren't there?' Jethu scratched his stubble. 'Our son was at his father-in-law's with his newly married wife two villages away from ours. The rioters took away my daughters. I don't know where my son and daughter-in-law are at the moment.'

'Jethu, I'm sure one day you'll be united with your family. You didn't see your wife and daughters being taken away. Hope for the best.'

'Like all refugees, the refugees in this boat also have their stories. I'm sure you have also your story.'

Gunen told him his story from the get-go and stared down at the river. Jethu, who was shivering with cold, almost huddled up with Gunen, who also felt cold, though not shivering like Jethu. The wind from across the river had blown cold to them. Despite the fog getting dense and noises made by the oars, he could notice the gloom intensifying around Jethu's face. He could hear Jethu weeping. Gunen looked up at the sky and knew from the positions of the stars that it was going to be midnight. The boat was sailing on.

'Where are we really going, Jethu?'

'To Assam.'

'Are you sure?'

'Yes.'

'Is it a nice place like East Pakistan?'

'Assam is full of forests. There are a variety of people. They eat a variety of food. The moist areas are infested with leech. A variety of leech lives in paddy fields too. This variety hides under grass blades to ambush its prey. Mosquitoes abound everywhere. There are only forests and forests. Every month earthquakes occur.'

'Can I speak Bengali in Assam?'

'There are many Bengali speaking people in Assam.'

'Are there Muslim people?'

'Yes.'

'Do they riot against Hindus?'

'I can't say. But I heard they're mild people. Most of the Muslims in Assam are migrants from East Pakistan. They're agrarian people like us. We're the same people divided by faiths.'

'Will the native people accept us?'

'They're gentle. Hospitable.'

'Where will the boat unload us?'

'The agents can tell it. Now let's go to sleep.'

Meghna sat up, started whimpering. 'Ask Masimoni to help me. I can't stand the pain.'

When Gunen sought Masimoni's help, Masimoni hurried up to Meghna and, before giving attention to her, ordered Gunen to immediately make a room with a sari, and to carry out her order, Gunen took Meghna's scarlet sari out of the bundle and made a room with the help of Jethu, who held the sari with his hands, as Gunen had held. Not able to know what was going to happen in there, Ginu kept standing, clutching at his father's shawl from behind and fighting off his tears. With outstretched hands, a young guy formed a barricade against the people, who wanted to see what had happened inside the sari-made room, out of which Meghna's labour cries she'd tried to keep in control were coming. People's mixed comments, intermittently drowned by the screeching oars, rose from all parts of the boat.

'What has happened to Ma?' Ginu asked.

'Nothing. Don't weep.'

*

At the crack of dawn, the people, who were woken by the cries of a newborn baby, got up with curiosities explicit in their eyes, and then the moment Gunen was going to open his mouth, Masimoni interrupted him with the gesture of her hand and satisfied their curiosities by giving them brief details of the baby and asked the over-enthusiastic women not to disturb the mother and the baby, who were in need of nursing care. They listened to Masimoni and went back to their places, inaudibly murmuring something to themselves. Gunen bullied Ginu into silence when he became persistent to see his sister. For Gunen and Jethu, it was almost a challenge to continue standing, raising their hands as posts of the sari-made room. Though Gunen didn't know if Jethu's endurance was on the wane, he realized his would crumble within a couple of minutes, and he felt he was no less interested than Ginu to have a look at his daughter. Then Masimoni told them to remove the sari and they promptly obeyed and sat beside Ginu sitting close to the baby, his fingertips delicately touching her reddish heels. Delighted like a victorious man, his lips compact, Gunen gazed down at the baby dazzling like a lump of gold in Meghna's lap, being washed by the tender light of the day; Meghna's face had received the dazzle of the baby. He took the baby from her and gently pressed her to his chest. From her face, he shifted his eyes to the golden sun liquefied in the river. She squirmed. He transferred her to Meghna's soft arms, not passing to Ginu nagging her to let him take the baby in his lap.

12

When the boat hit the bank of the tributary he didn't know when the boat had crossed, Gunen looked at the bright morning around: a few metres from there started a thin forest of tall trees; six men standing on the bank seemed to be waiting to welcome them. Giving a look at his son and then at his daughter in her mother's arm, Gunen helped them out of the boat after Jethu had got off.

Jethu couldn't tell if the boat had unloaded the people in Assam.

The agents ticked their names, hearing their responses; Gunen was the last man, and his number was 55, which meant there were 55 passengers—to be exact: 56, including the baby. The agents tallied their names with their records, then told them to break the lines and get ready to be led to a small hotel a mile away from there.

*

The hotel stood by the dirt road that passed through the forest, through which the glimpse of a little river was visible.

They filled the earthen pots by drawing water from the well, with a pulley, attached to a wheel tied to a parallel bar supported by two posts on either side of the well. They availed themselves of the toilet facilities in the open inside the forest divided into two sections—the right one for men: the left one for women.

*

They ate rice with *masur* lentil soup and bottle gourd curry. The new rice was sticky. It gave out a sweet flavour. They stood together to listen to an agent, who advised them to first exchange their money and then to carefully listen to the chief agent before starting their difficult phase of the journey through the forest. It was dense from that area.

Before joining the people, who had gone over to the money exchange counter, staffed by two young men, Gunen reached into his bag to take out the money Jahangir Alam had given him. He didn't find the money. The money was under the dagger in his bag. Extremely confused and upset, his head reeling and the energy from the food dwindling away, he looked towards the people and saw Jethu at the counter and walked up to him. His eyes went to the scrap of paper near Jethu's feet. He picked it up. It was Jahangir Alam's address. He walked close to Jethu and peeped over and saw Jethu counting out the money. He slipped out of that place, not able to bear the pain. Jethu had thought of him as a sitting duck. If Taimoor was a beast, Jethu was a jackal. Not only Jethu, but he must also avoid even Jethu's shadow. Hiding the storm blowing in his mind, he turned from there and found himself near his family.

Then, with his family, as he stood in the front line to listen to the chief agent, Jethu looked at him twice as if not looking and then turned his face away, seemingly trying to avoid him.

'You'll have to walk all night until you cross the border at early dawn. On the other side of the border, our Indian counterparts will receive you and our responsibility will end,' the chief agent said. 'We'll give you earthen pitchers to carry water. We filled the pitchers for you, with water from the tube-well. On the road, you won't find any tube-wells and get drinking water.' He pointed to the pitchers waiting to be lifted and carried. 'The sooner you can cross the border, the better for you. You're not safe in East Pakistan. You're safe only when you step into India.'

The sun was up. The misty cold of the morning was gone a little. The January wind was blowing sort of a gale from the direction of the river across the forest. The atmosphere was growing pleasant with new thrills of a new journey into a new land. But the cloud of gloominess that hovered over Gunen's mind devoured the thrills of pleasure he longed to enjoy. He would've become careful, and he wouldn't have trusted Jethu if his behaviour had dropped a hint of his wicked nature. Beguiled by Jethu's fake innocence, he decided to never consider a stranger trustworthy and dependable.

*

Their caravan set out on the journey to India. An agent was at its head; another one, at its tail. The agents asked them to strictly follow their instructions and walk fast so they could cross the hilly and deserted stretch of land before dusk fell.

The strong men in the families carried pitcherfuls of water. Gunen carried two pitcherfuls of water. The earthen pitchers hung from both ends of a bamboo bar horizontally placed on their shoulders. Masimoni's family, comprised of her husband, son, daughter-in-law, and two young daughters, were heading Gunen's family. Ginu was between Gunen and Meghna, who walked slowly with the baby in her arms. The pathways smelled of forest. There was tall grass on either side. Sometimes they passed through tall, yellow grass. In a grass-free area, they stopped and shook the dry blades off their clothes. All of them walked, watching their feet, and they didn't talk loudly. The baby's occasional cries startled the quiet of the area. Gunen liked hearing her cry; her cries helped him steer his attention away from Jethu. Though he'd tried to put his mind at rest about the money, he couldn't. For him twelve-thousand taka was a big amount. It would've helped him plan for his future. The loud cry of the baby broke the train of his thought, and he realized he'd forgotten when he'd slowed down and immediately increased his speed the way he could, keeping pace with Meghna, for whom Masimoni's family also walked slowly to let her keep pace with them. With the end of her sari, Meghna protected her daughter's face against the cold wind blowing from across that little river.

By the time they crossed a grassy area, the caravan stopped in a clearing at the foot of a hill. There were series of hills behind it.

'This is our last stop,' the agent, who led the caravan, said. 'We won't find a better place than this ahead. Those of you, who are hungry, may eat here.'

'Will you give us food?' a voice asked aloud.

'We gave you at the hotel what we could. Now you'll have to eat your own food. We gave you water. You can drink it. But use it carefully. You won't get drinking water anywhere until you cross the border. Going to India also, you may be required to drink this water.' The agent looked ahead. 'From here we'll have to become cautious. The East Pakistan police patrol this area. Sometimes robberies are also committed. If you're lucky, you won't encounter the police or the robbers. After thirty minutes, your risky journey will begin. We've chosen this path to avoid risk. Don't worry. We'll help you safely cross the border. From here, you must be careful with every step. It'll be a hilly area. In summer, venomous snakes appear. But luckily, it's winter. A blessing for all of us.'

'For how many days have you done this business?' a man from the crowd asked.

'We've been into this border-crossing business for a few years. So we're so experienced. We helped many Hindu families cross the border.'

'Don't you do trafficking?'

The agent sounded peeved about being asked that question, and his eyes searched for the voice. Taking off his stocking cap, he combed his hair with his fingers. 'Never dare to ask such nasty questions. Can you imagine where you'll end up if we leave you here? The police. The robbers. The forest animals. The hunger. The thirst. I can mention a long chain of enemies.'

'I'm sorry. I didn't intend to hurt you. It was just my curiosity.' The young guy stepped out of the crowd and sought the agent's forgiveness, raising his joined hands to his forehead in a salute.

The agent put on his cap. 'Divide yourselves into small groups. Walk without talking and making noises. Keep one another in sight. That's a strategy to avoid attention. The robbers and the police sense the movement and easily find the caravan. They're like predators. You can't say where and when they ambush you.'

Gunen touched the amulet. 'Protect her from the cold wind, Meghna.' He touched the baby's head and felt happy about the way Meghna had wrapped her in her old sweater and kept her to the warmth of her breasts. 'May I call our daughter Usha?'

'Yes. She was born at *usha*.' She gently kissed her forehead, Ginu standing, grabbing the end of her sari.

'We'll remain in one group. Never be separated,' said Masimoni before starting walking behind her son leading their group.

*

It was going to get dark when the groups marched into a new territory. Gunen looked up. No signs of when the moon would be out. The paths ahead were through bushes and trees. He led Meghna, shielding her and Usha against the leaves of the plants. Some plants were thorny. He'd once brushed his cheek against a thorny plant. Masimoni's two daughters and daughter-in-law were almost clinging to Masimoni. Except on Meghna's head, there were bundles, small or big, on everyone's head. Meso, Masimoni's sixty-plus or something husband, was at the tail of the line of their group. Masimoni's son, who was carrying water, led their group. Gunen didn't know the group Jethu was in, and he hadn't seen Jethu since the lead agent had finished giving them instructions.

None could walk fast.

Suddenly, Usha cried, breaking the silence. Gunen looked back and saw Meghna put her nipple in Usha's mouth so that she stopped crying. She was maybe hungry. She shouldn't have cried. Her cry would indicate their presence.

'How long will it take to cross the forest?' Meghna asked.

'Only the agents know,' Gunen answered.

'Where are the agents?'

'I don't know.'

'What'll happen to us if they leave us in the forest?'

'They took money from us to help us cross the border. They're responsible people. That's their business. They can never do this business if they cheat people. And they don't look like cheats.'

'But why don't we see them?'

'The people of the first group and the last group can see them. We're in the middle.'

'Can you go to the first group and see if he's there?'

'Crunches of feet on dry leaves! Listen,' Gunen whispered and looked left.

'Are they robbers or police?'

'The lead agent wants to tell us something.'

The lead agent motioned them to pick hiding places. The people dispersed in different directions in obedience to the agent. Gunen got the smell of impending danger. He felt his knees shake and blood run cold. He started breathing hard. Not wasting a moment to take out his dagger, he looked right and saw a ridge, and as he walked ahead, he saw a narrow gorge down the ridge covered by bushy plants. A suitable hiding place. With her family, Masimoni hid in the cluster of bushes a few feet away from the ridge when Gunen hid in the gorge, with his family. Gunen would've been able to see them in the filtered moonlight unless there had been darkness from the plants and trees and the gorge's serrated walls.

When noises resembling grunts of pain drifted to Gunen's ears from a few feet away from where they were, he erected his ears, concern orbiting his face. Though sure the robbers or the police wouldn't be able to see them in there, he got afraid as he thought of Usha; if she cried, they would immediately come over to the ridge and find them; so the only way to avoid that problem was put her mother's nipple in her mouth. He knew she cried when she got hungry or felt discomfort. Could he ever imagine that a one-day-old baby too can cause a security problem? She was now sleeping on Meghna's lap, and Meghna was crouching down, leaning protectively over her, and Ginu huddling close to Meghna. In their eyes was panic slightly visible in the faint light of the moon on the shoulders of the hills.

'Take care of Usha. If she cries, they'll come to find us. They loot valuables and snatch away girls. You're also beautiful. You don't look like you gave birth to a baby last night,' Gunen whispered as low as possible.

Suddenly, people started shouting and crying. Ears pricked for the noises, Gunen looked at Meghna stiffening with fear and leaning down into the grass, and

Ginu crawling up to him, their eyes fixed on the dagger in his right hand. Gunen stood up and thoughtfully peered through the gathering fog: there was none; the fog would give them cover; it should thicken as soon as it could.

Bullying, crying, shouting, and loud voices begging for kindness stirred the forest and echoed in the hills. Gunen heard the voices of the agents trying to defend the people, and when, within minutes, their voices were muffled, he got prepared to fight and resolved to fight them to save the two families if they came up.

He had an amulet on his arm.

'Are they coming over to this place?' Meghna asked.

'Don't talk. Just take care of Usha. She must not cry. Feed her if she wakes up,' Gunen replied.

'What will we do if they come?' Meghna let Ginu put his head on her lap.

'Keep silent. They're coming.' Gunen heard Jethu's plaintive voice. He stood up and saw two robbers beating Jethu while dragging him towards the ridge.

'Where have you hidden your bundle? Take us to your bundle,' a robber said.

'I have lost my bundle. I had nothing in my bundle except some old clothes,' Jethu said.

'Tell us where your bundle is.'

'I didn't have any money in my bundle. I'm a poor man.'

The robbers again started beating Jethu with their

lathis. He didn't admit he had money on him or in his bag. He was crying. They didn't stop beating him. As the other robber took out his machete and got ready to strike Jethu's neck, Jethu led them to his bundle.

Usha cried out.

'Put your nipple in her mouth,' Gunen said, looking at Usha. 'The robbers may come to find us here. I'll go out and prevent them from coming over to the gorge. Stay in the gorge until I return.'

'Be careful. They're ferocious.' Meghna lay flat on the grass.

Gunen came out of the gorge and hunkered behind the boulder on his left and when he stood up to see where the robbers were, he heard Masimoni shout for help and, not waiting to decide what to do or what not to do, he flung himself in front of the robbers to defend Meso and Masimoni struggling to extricate their daughters and daughter-in-law from their hands. He identified the robust robber as Muttu and the short robber with thick moustache as Moustache. Muttu forced Masimoni's son to surrender their bundles and money. Not satisfied with the booties, Muttu grabbed the eldest girl's hand, and before Muttu could drag her into the trees and vanish, he faced Muttu, his dagger ready in his hand. Muttu charged him with his sword, and he twisted back into a loop so he could attack Muttu from behind, and then, just glancing at the gorge, where his wife, son, and daughter were hiding, he swerved right, swooped on Muttu, and pushed the dagger into Muttu's back when Muttu bent down. Muttu straightened himself, scowled at him, and not long before Muttu staggered ahead, he jumped right to avoid the sword aimed at his belly and to let Muttu come ahead from near Masimoni and her daughter. Muttu cursed him in foul language and charged at him, baring his teeth in anger and pain. Without wasting a moment, he ducked down to avoid the swipe of Muttu's sword before thrusting his dagger into Muttu's belly so that Muttu fell to the tree, the head hard against the scraggy rock. On seeing that, Moustache left the eldest girl, picked up the sword, and chased him into the foggy patches of darkness above the ridge. He touched his amulet, gained confidence in his power, and stood behind a tree on the ridge. Moustache followed him up to the tree and as soon as Moustache showed up in the fog-filtered moonlight, he jumped from the shoulder of the ridge to lodge himself straight close at the foot of the tree Moustache was standing under. He thanked his good luck when he realized that the hard swipe of Moustache's sword would have severed his head off his shoulder unless he'd swept right and bent down at the appropriate moment. Before Moustache took another attempt, he'd speedily stoop-walked and thrust the dagger into his abdomen. He'd thrust it twice. Fighting a spasm of hysteria, Moustache fell on his back, twitched, flailed, and thumped his legs, while trying to breathe hard, the sword lying close by his stiffening right hand, the stream of his blood reddening the grass. Frazzled in the extreme, he heaved a deep sigh; he'd been compelled to commit that crime; he didn't feel any compunction about it. Then, when he went over to the gorge and didn't find his family in there, he hurried back to where Masimoni and her family had hidden, and not finding them there, he called out to Meghna and Ginu and then to Meso and Masimoni. None responded. Anxiety and tension making him thirsty, he came to the place where they'd left the pitchers. They'd taken away their pitchers, leaving his pitchers and bundle.

By tilting a pitcher, he poured water in the cup of his right hand and drank from it. Disheartened and tired, he started searching for them. Had they scattered into the forest in search of escape routes when he was fighting the robbers? Had they also got separated from one another? If they'd got separated, it'd be difficult for them to get united. He'd be able to cross the border alone. But it might be difficult for them to do so. Worried, he walked into the forest, and before going far from where he'd got separated from them, he looked back a few times to know if he'd taken the right direction. It was difficult to walk through the bushes, rocks, and roots underfoot. But he didn't let those problems sit in his head. Now there was nothing in his head except the thought of going out of that area and making sure of whether they'd been able to safely cross the border.

Gunen walked on, looking back time and again. As he tripped and fell forward, the pitchers slipped from his shoulder and broke into shards, the water flowing through the yellow grass peeping from behind the small stones past the rock he'd grazed his right knee on. Glancing at the shards lying strewn, he sat up with some effort and looked at the blood oozing from his right knee. Where had they gone? Were they following the right direction? Now Usha should cry. He tried to rise to his feet. But he couldn't. He repeated his efforts. He wondered if he'd be able to rise and walk like before or if his legs would cooperate with him. Concerned about his condition, he minutely examined his kneecap. It was beyond his capacity to diagnose the injury. He looked at the trees; he would've felt colder than he felt at present if not surrounded by the trees. He looked up and saw the moon's brightness had dimmed the twinkle of the stars. Failing to rise to his feet, he touched the amulet so he could get the courage and strength he now needed most. Some rest would help him. So, before lying down, he placed his bag near the bundle beside the boulder and used the bag as a pillow, keeping his head on the side of its mouth, because in the bottom of the bag was the knife.

Jackals' yells—they were maybe somewhere nearby—woke him up, and he fumbled around and took a few seconds to realize that he had come to normal. He touched his kneecap, tried to stretch his leg, and managed to sit up. He remembered the robbers, who had committed extreme atrocities on many people, and from his mind, banished the regret about doing an act of inhumanity, which he'd been constrained to do in urgent response to the situation.

Feeling determined to find his family as soon as possible, he rose to his feet, touched the amulet yet again and started walking along the narrow path, unaware of the distance. He thought about whether he'd be required to walk all night or till noon, the next day to cross the border and whether he was following the right path in the right direction. Now he decided not to think of his family; the thought of his family made him feel drained of energy he needed to find them anyhow. Despite the fog, he could see the path and assumed Meghna—Usha certainly in her arms and Ginu holding her sari she had on—hadn't found much difficulty in following Masimoni's family if they'd walked the path he was now walking.

The insects had risen long ago. No animals were seen. No animals were heard except jackals.

13

Gunen stumbled over the border stone. He looked east, saw the sky show the sign of dawn, bowed down, and then he made obeisance to East Pakistan and took a pinch of earth to smear it on his forehead, the pain of being estranged from his family pounding his heart and making his eyes fill with tears he couldn't remember when he'd last wiped off. Feeling forlorn and empty-hearted, as he wondered if they'd been able to cross the border and where they were at present, a dark cloud of uncertainty formed in his mind's sky.

Resolute to search for his family, he crossed the border and dropped to his knees and made obeisance to India like he'd made to East Pakistan. Had his family been with him, he would've sung a song of freedom and danced with Usha in his arms and Ginu sitting astride his shoulders, holding on to his head to steady his balance. But luck had conspired against him, robbed him of his happiness.

*

Tired to the bones, once Gunen reached a refugee camp, a group of six volunteers had greeted him before one of them led him to a tent and offered him their limited hospitality.

Though he required a sound sleep to regain his energy for the next phase of the journey, he left his bag and bundle in charge of the volunteers, and then the instant he stepped out of the camp to look for his wife and children, he heard a woman crying in the camp around two hundred feet away at the fringe of the forest down the gravel road behind.

He went over to the camp and saw her lying on her stomach, her face in the bowl of her hands. She was crying non-stop. Unable to stand the spasm of her sorrow, he sat down and touched her back to calm her. He helped her sit up, and when he wanted to know the reason why she was crying like that, she told him the reason: the robbers had severed her husband's head in front of her eyes; they'd also wanted to kill her when she'd tried to save her daughters; her husband had fought the robbers to save her daughters, but couldn't succeed; after severing his head, they'd perforated his body with their spears when her daughters had resisted; she'd seen her daughters jump off the crest of the small hill as the robbers had tried to capture them; some people had carried her to the camp; now there was nothing with her except her sorrow.

'Don't weep, Kaki. I'll take you with me.'

Staring into his eyes, she started howling.

There were some other people, who had either been robbed of their properties or lost their people. Some couldn't say what had happened to their women and daughters. When he looked back, hearing footfalls, he saw Jethu standing and before he could turn his face away to get up to leave, Jethu grasped his hand and pulled him down to where he was sitting beside Kaki.

Jethu sat down. 'I stole your money. Your money saved my life. If they hadn't got the money from me, they would've killed me. Only the lucky ones who could hide in time have survived.' He wiped his eyes. 'All of us are unlucky people.'

'You betrayed my trust. That pained me.'

'I was afraid of begging on the street. I wanted to start a small business with the money. Twelve thousand takas is a big amount for a poor old man like me.'

'You didn't think for me.'

'You're young man. You can find a job.' Jethu tightly held Gunen's hands. 'I seek your forgiveness.'

Gunen freed his hands, nodded, and smiled before turning from him to find himself in the camp, where he'd kept his bag and bundle. When he saw those people were gone, he felt like falling from a tree to a rock and wondered where they could go in about thirty minutes, whether there was a vehicle near somewhere, which he hadn't seen or cared to see. He sprinted up to the volunteers, who told him that those people had been shifted to another camp and from there they would be shifted to Tura, where Indian Government had built permanent camps to shelter the refugees, and except that, they couldn't give him any further information about the location of the camp they had been shifted to at present. He slumped down on the patch of grass near the legs of the bench on his left and looked at the clouds negotiating the horizon.

'Wait for the next bus. If you're lucky you'll meet your family,' the volunteer, who oversaw Gunen's bag and bundle, said.

After they'd wandered away, he went over to the bench and, too tired and sleepy to keep his eyes open, he placed the bundle under it and lay down, using the bag as a pillow, and within minutes he closed his eyes, he went to sleep.

*

The volunteer, who woke him up, served him hodgepodge and *labra*, a kind of curry prepared with mixed vegetables. After eating, when he drank a bottle of water, Jethu and Kaki came to mind, and he hastily went from there to find them in that camp.

They were also gone.

'A bus took them away to a camp in Tura,' the man, who was cleaning the camp, said when Gunen wanted to know about them.

Gunen found himself near the bench in front of the camp he'd been first led into. Now that no volunteers were there, he became apprehensive about moving out of this place because he was a stranger in that locality. In the camps, which were now empty of people, stray dogs were searching for leftovers in the used platters made from leaves of *sal* trees. A dog pissed on the torn pieces of clothes near the platters. To take some rest and regain some energy and feel fresh, he walked up to the bench and sat down, his left hand stretched on the bag. He looked at the forest that began from the rows of trees down the camps. The forest was behind the camps at the foot of the hill, which stood detached from the series of small and big hills.

The dog, which wandered up to him, got Gunen to remember Appon, and, when Gunen patted the dog's head, the dog twirled his tail right and Gunen knew the dog felt happy. Then another dog came up, and Gunen patted his head too. They lay down.

Gunen had never felt so left alone before. 'If you don't feel you're alone, you're never alone.' He looked towards the forest and the hills.

14

2018

Gunen had two valid certificates: citizenship and refugee; the citizenship certificate was issued by the Government of Assam and the refugee certificate, by the Tura Refugee Camp in 1964. But he had no legacy data. It was mandatory for the successful submission of the NRC application. To obtain the legacy data, he'd moved from one cyber café to another one and come back home frustrated again and again.

At the make-shift NRC office, Gunen couldn't properly answer Mr Barman's questions because fear and nervousness got him to get confused, and despite this problem, he approached only Mr Barman he was comfortable with. The other five officers designate played ribald jokes on him. They treated him as an illegal settler and laughed off his answers to their irrelevant questions. The lanes and alleys before his eyes closed when Mr Barman declined to touch his application without the legacy data.

'I can't go against the computer crammed with the systems that scrutinized and processed the applications,' Mr Barman said.

Mr Barman was a dark-complexioned man in his fifties. He was tall and handsome. He walked with long steps, keeping his body straight. His amiable behaviour and cordial smile added an extra layer to his personality. Those who knew that he was in the habit of chewing paans and drinking six to eight litres of water a day, called him a paan-addict and hydro-maniac, for fun.

*

From the door of the NRC office, Gunen glanced at those officers sideways, stepped in, and stood at Mr Barman's table. He had set his worn-out file near the paperweight on the table before he sat in the chair across from Mr Barman. Then, the instant he put the packet of six paans and two two-litre bottles of Bisleri water between the file and the paperweight, Mr Barman withdrew his eyes from the computer screen.

'I drink more than six to eight litres of water a day. Right. But I'm not a hydro-maniac. Do you also think of me as a hydro-maniac? A paan-addict? Like those good-for-nothing people?' Mr Barman let his scowl pierce Gunen's face. 'I'm helpless.'

'Please just another attempt, sir.' Gunen stood up, folding hands at his chest.

'Never ask me again to try to upload your application. This is my last attempt. I'm too powerless to help you. Next time if you come up without the legacy data, I won't even look at your application. I can't go against the computer. It's packed with the systems that scrutinize and process the applications.' Mr Barman took the packet of *paans* and the bottles from the table and put them in its bottom drawer.

*

After returning home, Gunen threw the file onto his bed, went into the kitchen, poured a glass of water from the jug, and drank up the water. He took off his shirt and wiped the sweat from his body. With the file, he sat in his old wooden chair at his old table, opened the file, and ran the tip of his index finger over the names: Gunen Sarkar, Meghna Sarkar, Gyanpada Sarkar Ginu, and Usha Sarkar. He closed the file, put it in the trunk.

Now that the legacy problem had turned his world upside down, he started to think of his world, like a man on the verge of insanity, and he felt so when he imagined being locked up in a detention camp and then being deported from Assam. Like the other refugees at Refugee Gaon, he'd also always thought he would forever live in Assam, which he had accepted as his motherland. Though his mother tongue was Bengali, he'd declared Assamese as his mother tongue, without fakeness, without cunning, without any intention to play tricks to get identity benefit. He could've declared Assamese as his first language too, but he hadn't done so, and it was because of his gratefulness to Assam, to the Assamese, who had sympathized with the refugees. Panicked by the nightmare of being outnumbered by the uninterrupted flow of exodus of foreign nationals, the Assamese felt their demography, economy, culture, and language threatened, and visualized living a life of fear and subjugation destitute of safety and security. In East Pakistan, like all other refugees, Gunen had also experienced a life of fear and subjugation. That was one of the reasons why he criticized the Bengali, who didn't tend to think as he thought and held those types of people responsible for creating the history of conflict between the Assamese and the Bengali bestowed with many common characteristics.

Appon was looking up at his face. He looked hungry.

After giving Appon two stale rotis he'd kept away in the kitchen cabinet, he carried the chair to the veranda and sat down, his legs on the bamboo stool. His eyes travelling with the cirrus in the high noon sky, he transported his mind to the past.

Without the help of Tongko Borbora—he was the headmaster of Lorigaon High School and his mentor at Refugee Gaon—he would've ended up nowhere. Tongko Borbora had filled in his NRC application and attached the documents Gunen had produced. It was because of Tongko Borbora's sincere efforts and care that he now could present himself as a literate young man. Tongko Borbora had taught him Assamese, English, and some mathematics and science. Tongko Borbora, who wore a bushy moustache almost hiding his upper lip, was tall and robust, and his whole body was covered with hair that stuck out at his sternum through the neck of his *churiya* and at his hands through its cuffs. He preferred to wear dhoti and *churiya*. A homemade *gamosa* draped his shoulders, when he went out, and when at home, he preferred to wear a large homemade *gamosa* and half-sleeved vest. His rough voice and prying eyes showed he was an angry type, but he wasn't that angry; injustice and dishonesty triggered his anger he sometimes failed to keep in control. Tongko Borbora appointed Gunen as a farmhand to work in his crop fields when Gunen asked him to give him a job. As a sincere and honest farmhand, Gunen won his confidence within a month, and it was his good luck that Tongko Borbora never increased Gunen's workload. Tongko Borbora admiringly watched Gunen swiftly pulling out saplings and planting them in the muddy crop field.

In contrast with her husband, Mrs Borbora was a short woman—hardly five feet. She was beautiful and fair-complexioned though slightly overweight. Her musical voice and smile pleased the people she talked to. She was kind-hearted. Whenever he got a chance to talk about his wife, Tongko Borbora said that her mind was as clean as the inside of a coconut. The Assamese cuisine achieved a new dimension in her kitchen she never liked to allow anyone to enter except her daughters—they had two sons and two daughters. Mrs Borbora gave him rice and vegetables or whatever was there in her kitchen so he could eat at night, after coming back home.

Whenever he sat down to eat at night, Meghna, Ginu, and Usha appeared in his mind and inspired him to mentally talk to them to forget the taste of the food. They gave him a heavy breakfast. Sometimes, they gave him *bora* rice with milk and banana; sometimes, homemade *idli* he preferred to call vapcakes.

Like in East Pakistan, at Refugee Gaon too, Gunen never demanded anything from the people he helped. People loved him and depended on him. To make them feel happy, he tried as best as he could. Not a single refugee had bought a plot of land at Refugee Gaon. It was their opportunity to settle at Refugee Gaon.

In search of Meghna, Ginu, and Usha, he'd almost scoured Assam since his arrival. He got nothing but failure and frustration. He wondered if they'd also faced the same problems as he'd faced.

He needed money to build a better house than that built by the Government for free. He needed his own land and cattle to live the way he'd lived in East Pakistan. To fulfil those small dreams, he worked as an assistant of a carpenter and a fisherman respectively.

At the carpenter's furniture house, which was near Hatigaon Market around four kilometres from Refugee Gaon, he gathered a load of experiences by mixing with drunkards, gamblers, womanizers, goons, and cheats. He often thought of stopping working for that carpenter. But he couldn't. He was paid well. The carpenter drank regularly. in the evening, his friends came and drank till 10:30 pm. Against his mind, Gunen carried out the carpenter's order to buy wine in the wine shop around a hundred metres from the furniture house. The carpenter sympathized with Gunen and gave him extra money so he could search for his family in new places. He often advised Gunen to drink to mitigate his suffering from the separation from his family. He finally accepted the carpenter's advice. Wine had made him lose his money and integrity.

He searched for women, who searched for customers at night. That was because of the company of the carpenter's depraved friends.

He unexpectedly fell in love with the carpenter's daughter. Her name was Jeuti. She was about five feet three inches tall, fair-complexioned. When she smiled, it looked as though her teeth sowed pearls around. Her smooth and bright skin felt like rose petals to his touch. He pictured his future in her large eyes beautified by the long lashes. In the backyard, flooded by moonlight, once he discovered her big and firm breasts, he became speechless, and then the subsequent discovery of her round and uplifted buttocks and round and smooth thighs made him so excited he couldn't help pulling her against his erection, in less than a minute. He let her explore his starving virility and masculinity with her long fingers, enjoying being warmed by her breaths on his chest and shoulder. The way her body responded showed that she was as eager as him to plunge into the whirlpool of lovemaking. Not wasting the precious time on more foreplay and breathing in her fragrance, he extricated his head from between her thighs as she bent down. While sucking her breasts, he gently bit her nipples, and she pushed his head away, agitating the moonlight with her noisy breaths. He understood her indication and got lost in the final phase of the romantic session. After about two or three months of such quick lovemaking, one morning, she threw a stone chip at his feet when he was milking the cow. The chip was wrapped in her love letter. That was her first and last love letter. The letter made him collapse to his knees just the moment he finished reading it: her parents had become aware of their affair and that they had planned to marry her off as soon as possible. Upset in the extreme, that day, he came back home in the afternoon. He didn't cook and spent the night without eating, thinking of what he should do. He realized it wouldn't be possible for him to live without her. At the wee hours, he suddenly decided to convince her of the necessity for elopement. Sitting on the concrete bench under the banyan tree, he waited for her. At exactly 9:30 am, when he saw her come towards the tree the dirt road ran past, he walked over and told her about his decision. She wanted to know how he'd earn his living to support his family, as a stranger in a new place. Keeping silent for a minute, he held her left hand in his and touched it to his forehead to mean he'd do any job to earn a living, following the dictates of destiny. She agreed.

After two days, they eloped. But luck wasn't in their favour. They were caught when they were waiting for a bus, under the banyan tree. Later, in the carpenter's outhouse, while receiving severe beating, Gunen heard that he'd be put in a gunny sack alive and thrown into the Brahmaputra River. They tied him to a post in the outhouse and waited for the night to obey the carpenter's order. The carpenter's wife, who was aware of the conspiracy, freed Gunen and advised him to hide in an unknown place so the carpenter's people couldn't find him. He regretted meeting with Jeuti at the secret rendezvous. He was responsible for making her yield to his amorous caress and for allowing him to explore her to the core and quench her thirst while quenching his. After his starving libido had fed on her abundant fluidity, he'd magically forgotten his family and promised to spend his remaining life with Jeuti. He shouldn't have done so.

After coming back to his house, he met Jagat Ghose and told him about the affair before depositing the key and the trunk with Jagat; Jagat, the owner of the Mango Hotel and Restaurant, was his only reliable friend at Refugee Gaon. He asked Jagat to take care of the house, during his absence.

Then he'd worked as a Muslim fisherman's assistant for two years. They fisherman treated him as his younger brother. The fisherman taught him how to row a boat, how to catch hilsa fish in the Brahmaputra River, and how to handle customers while selling fish at market, in his presence or absence. The fisherman trusted him more than his two sons, who often stole money to squander on gambling. When he thought he couldn't live happily except at Refugee Gaon—he'd lived away from his village for two years—he took the fisherman's permission to leave for his village.

'If you smell any trouble there, come back to this house. Our door is always open to you,' the fisherman said when he came to the bus stop to see him off.

Returning to his house, he found everything okay except the garden, where dried stumps of rose plants sadly peeped through weeds and creepers.

With Tongko Borbora's help, Gunen bought six bighas of fertile land, a kilometer from Refugee Gaon. He brought with him twenty-one thousand rupees. His first earning was twenty-six thousand rupees he'd left in his trunk deposited with Jagat. Jagat lent him fourteen thousand rupees to help him buy a pair of bullocks and a milk cow. After three years, he had bought another six bighas and established himself as a rich cultivator.

Gunen withdrew his mind from the past to concentrate on the present. Would he fail to find his family like he'd failed to find the brown cow? Frustration would've crippled him unless he'd Old Gypsy's amulet on his right upper arm.

He remembered his parents, leaned forward, lifted the lungi he had on up to his right thigh, and ran his fingertips over the dark horizontal mark, a gift of his father's stick, which would've given him more such gifts that morning unless his mother had forcibly snatched it from his hand and thrown it away to the foot of the bottle gourd creepers.

The memory of the brown cow brought tears to his eyes.

He picked two clods of earth from beneath the window looking out his small garden and threw them at the neighbour's tom cat and the squirrel to drive them away when he saw the tom cat get ready to jump up and catch the squirrel, which had come down the guava tree and sat on the top of the fence's post.

He came in.

15

Gunen had been used to opening his NRC file. After reading the Sunday supplement of the *Agradoot*, he put it on the table. He drank a glass of water. It was a hot day. Wiping his lips, he sat in his chair. Because he couldn't submit his NRC application, he'd forgotten everything except the NRC, which didn't let him sleep as he'd slept before, and when unable to sleep, he came out of the room and walked the dirt street that had run along past his house. Going to bed, even after walking, he remained awake, rolling from side to side, the NRC gnawing at the calm of his mind.

Interrupting the stream of Gunen's thought, Appon wandered in from nowhere, licking his muzzle over and over, his stare fixed on Gunen's face, and his tail down. He didn't stand on his hind legs to embrace Gunen—he used to do so to give Gunen the message that he was hungry. Appon looked worried.

'Don't worry about my legacy, Appon. If I'm put in a detention camp or deported, I'll take you with me. If they don't let me do that, I'll throw myself into the Brahmaputra River.'

After coming back to Refugee Gaon, Gunen had felt lonely like an ostracized man; his loneliness would've continued till today unless he'd happened to find Appon, who had lessened his loneliness, like a trustworthy friend. He'd picked him from beside a dusty shrub down their dirt street, where he was whining. He'd named him Appon.

Appon licked his muzzle.

'You're lucky you don't have to worry about your legacy. Do you know your legacy? No. I don't know either. You forgot long ago the place wherefrom I'd picked you. You're better than me, Appon. And you're lucky for another reason. That's you have your lover. She comes to see you and you go to see her. I wish you the best for your romantic life. But never bring her into my room in my absence. She is not as disciplined as you are.' He recalled that Appon. 'That Appon didn't have any lovers, like you.'

Gunen opened the trunk and took out the letter he'd failed to post, for fear of being discovered that he was in the village of that fisherman; the village had offered him a safe hiding place and source of earning. So before going to read the letter in Assamese aloud, he mentally thanked Tongko Borbora, for teaching him how to read and write— before starting to read or write he used to mentally thank his "Tongko-sir"; he had nothing to give his "Tongko-sir" but his thanks.

'Dear Meghna, I love you. I'll love you like this forever. You make me feel as though I have a big support I can lean on and use to break my fall if I happen to stumble while trying to get over the hurdles. Sometimes I picture myself as a small bird flying in the sky and suddenly landing on your outstretched, supportive hand, being chased by a terror in the guise of a big

hunting bird. Sometimes I picture myself dropping to my knees at your feet, crying for your support you can never decline to offer. I had confidence in you. But I wonder if I am worthy of you, if you will love me like you loved me when you will know about my debauchery ...'

The letter in his hand, he thoughtfully looked at the trunk chained to the leg of his bed. In it was his actual legacy. Wouldn't they laugh at the bottle and the dagger if he produced them to the officers and claimed those things to be his legacy? He decided to show them to Mr Barman in his house and wondered why the idea to show them to him hadn't struck his mind before. With the bunch of keys from his drawer, he opened the trunk, took out the bottle and the dagger, placed them on the table, opened the bottle, looked at the soil, and sniffed: the same smell. He lifted the dagger, examined its sharpness, and then, the dagger and the bottle in each hand, he thought if Mr Barman would consider them as his legacy when they would be produced. He stared at the dagger and remembered how he'd saved his and Masimoni's families.

The way Appon licked his lips showed he was very hungry, and his hunger got Gunen to feel hungrier than he was. He got up, went into the kitchen, and found two stale rotis in the steel pan kept in the dresser he never forgot to lock when he went out. But today he'd forgotten to lock it. It was his good luck that the front-door neighbour's cat hadn't sneaked into the kitchen through the window he'd forgotten to close too. He was growing unmindful of the important things, but he didn't lose his mind like some people had lost, unable to apply for the NRC.

Inspired by the roti's smell, Appon stood on his hind legs, embraced him, and snatched a roti from his outstretched hand. Appon quickly ate it up, then lay prostrate like in a prayer, his hungry look glinting with his desire to get more. Gunen tore his roti in two equal parts and shared a part with Appon.

Jagat had called him twice as he was in the NRC office. He hadn't taken the call. Jagat had called him, because he hadn't given him the milk, which was lying in the bucket in his room. His two cows gave him five litres of milk. Before going to the kitchen to cook for him and Appon, he called Jagat and told him he'd give him the milk in the afternoon.

*

From the Mango Restaurant, Gunen went to Taki Beel to the north of Refugee Gaon. To take in the view of the hills on its eastern and western sides, he sat on the patch of grass. In the rains, the Brahmaputra flooded the *beel*. It was the biggest beel in the district and abounded with varieties of fish. When he lifted his eyes from the hills and turned right, he saw Appon roaming the bank and searching for something. Not disturbing Appon, he walked up to the hyacinth clusters and plucked two hyacinth flowers. He returned to the patch of grass and sat down. He remembered his cast net he'd thrown into the water beside hyacinth clusters, where he knew fish used to collect. He'd felt excited when the fish under the net had made the rope in his hand tremble. The carp fish he'd caught last year with his cast net weighed five kilograms. Sitting on the bank of the beel couldn't calm his mind like before; the NRC problem had constantly taxed his brains.

He decided to visit Mr Barman in the evening to show him what he thought as his legacy. He got up to return home, being followed by Appon.

16

At 6:48 pm, Gunen knocked on the corrugated tin sheet of the gate of Mr Barman's house surrounded by tin sheets. Appon was with him. The house was on a dirt street running along the bank of the river that remained dry except in the rainy season. He stopped and kept looking at the two drunkards until they vanished at the point where the narrow path curved out—they'd waddled past, supporting each other; they'd called Appon names, criticized the NRC, and cursed it. Not able to satisfy his curiosity about whether they'd also suffered the NRC problem, he reached into the plastic bag and fingered the smoothness of the two bottles of whisky and decided to buy two more bottles if those two bottles failed to make them get drunk. He knocked louder than before, and when no response came, he searched for a hole, found one on the sheet-wall, peeped in, and saw Mr Barman standing in the patches of darkness under the tree; he was wearing a vest and a lungi and holding a stick in his right hand. He knocked again. Appon stood on his hind legs and started scratching the sheet and stopped barking the moment Mr Barman came straight in front of the hole.

'Please open the gate, sir.'

'Who're you here to disturb me in the evening?'

'I'm Gunen, sir. Please open the gate.'

'Why have you come here?'

'Please open the gate, sir.'

As soon as Mr Barman opened the gate, they stepped in.

'Is it your dog?'

'He's my Appon, sir.'

'Does it bite?'

'He's my friend.'

'Does it bite?'

'He is as gentle as I am.'

*

Mr Barman sat in the wooden chair. Gunen pulled the plastic chair and sat down across from him and put his bag on the table, glancing at *The Assam Tribune* lying in the space next to the stack of NRC files.

'May I know the purpose of your visit?' Mr Barman ran his fingers from the chin down the Adam's apple to the sternum.

'I've come here to show you my legacy, sir.'

'Could you get the data?'

'No, I couldn't.'

'You confuse me.'

Gunen took the bottle and dagger from his bag. He placed them on the table.

Mr Barman started up. 'Why the dagger?'

Not caring to answer the question, Gunen took out the bottles of whisky and placed them near the bottle containing the fistful of soil. Mr Barman became speechless, and from the movement of his lips, Gunen figured that he struggled to find words to speak.

'I've come here with a good intention, sir. If you're afraid of the dagger, you may please take it in your hand.'

'No, no. I'm not afraid of it.' Mr Barman tried to smile. 'Do you think this bottle and this dagger your legacy?'

'Yes, sir.'

'I don't understand.'

Gunen put the bottle down on the centre table Mr Barman was sitting at.

'What's there in the bottle?'

'My legacy.' Gunen opened the bottle.

Mr Barman looked in it. 'Soil?'

'Yes, sir.'

'Is the dagger also your legacy?'

Nodding yes, when Gunen handed him the dagger, he scrutinized the butt before running his right fingertips along the blade.

'You whet it regularly?'

'Once or twice a month, sir. It's my ancestral dagger.'

'So it's your legacy?'

'I consider it as my legacy.'

'What about the soil in the bottle?'

Gunen told Mr Barman the story about the soil in the bottle and the dagger. He also told him how he'd saved his and Masimoni's families from robbers. Mr Barman's stare at Gunen's face didn't waver. Gunen set the bottles of *MacDowell's* whisky on the centre table.

'Just a minute,' Mr Barman said in English and went in.

Gunen looked at Appon sitting on the veranda. He'd kept the door partially open so they could see each other. Within ten or twelve minutes, Mr Barman came back with two empty plates and a bowl. In the bowl was mutton stew.

'Just a minute,' Mr Barman said in English, waving his hand, and went in again. He brought snacks, two wine glasses, two spoons, a jugful of water, and ice cubes. He sat down. 'Who'll open the bottle?'

'You'll open it, sir. It's for your honour.'

With a smile, Mr Barman opened a bottle and asked Gunen to fill the glasses. Gunen obeyed. Mr Barman delicately dropped ice cubes in the glasses. They clinked and cheered. Gunen wished for his legacy data; Mr Barman, for his ability to help Gunen. After two pegs, they became slow. Mr Barman put a piece of meat in his mouth. Gunen looked at Appon. He was looking at the plates, licking his muzzle. Gunen tore a piece of paper and offered him two pieces of meat on it.

Mr Barman got angry. He picked the rod from under the table. Gunen prevented him from discharging his anger on Appon. The meat in his mouth, Appon went away to a safe distance.

'Get out. Get out, right off. Did you think I cooked meat for your dog?' Mr Barman threw the bottles into the courtyard.

Gunen followed him into the room and picked up his bag. Not standing to watch how Mr Barman was trembling with anger and hear how badly the abusive comments were streaming out of his mouth, Gunen picked up the bottles, came out of the house, stumbled onto the street, and started walking swiftly, the wine slightly in his head and Appon at his heels. He climbed the slope, took long breaths, and turned towards the street to Refugee Gaon.

*

Gunen stopped singing the Bengali folk song about a weeping stork in a trap and hid behind the hedge when he saw a man waddling along the street. Appon started barking. After the man had disappeared into the darkness, Gunen came out, entered the compound, and stepped onto the veranda. He put down his bag and the bottle near the post and opened the door with the key from the pocket of his pants. Just entering the room, he threw the bottle and the bag on the bed and lay down, and then, when he recalled his failure from the beginning to the end, the stork weeping after falling into the trap appeared like a picture before his mind's eyes and got him to compare his NRC problem with a trap. Though he knew he wasn't weeping, he touched the corners of his eyes to confirm if they were dry. From the veranda, Appon ran into the room through the open door and began to bark again. Gunen assumed that Appon had perhaps seen that drunkard and to know who he was and whether he was in the compound, Gunen went out and saw him standing down the veranda.

He was Sujan Das, Michael Munda's bosom friend; Sujan and Michael used to drink together to get drunk. *Laopani*, a variety of country liquor, was their favourite drink. Gunen helped Sujan walk up the steps of the veranda.

'I'll stay the night here. I won't go home.' Sujan sat in the chair. 'My wife and my son and daughter didn't allow me to enter the house.' A faint smile flickered across his lips when he looked at the bottle lying propped against the bag.

Gunen removed the bottle from there. He knew he wouldn't be able to prevent Sujan from drinking. Unmindful of whether it was a bed or a piece of furniture, Sujan vomited, when he drank much.

Despite his best efforts, he finally yielded to Sujan's pressure and drank together until they got drunk. While drinking they discussed their hardships, the women, and their husbands in their villages, and Gunen criticized Jagat's moustache and parrot nose, including his closely cropped hair, and boasted of being more handsome than Jagat, who was taller and more muscular than him. Though he was clean-shaven all along, nowadays there was stubble on his cheeks, and he told people he had no time to look at his face because of being constantly busy searching for his legacy data. Luck had favoured Sujan, who had successfully submitted his NRC application with the help of his son. Sujan's wife and sons and daughter were not bad people; his wife had repeatedly asked Sujan to stop drinking and doing fish business since when her eldest son got a job as a teacher at Refugee Gaon High School. But he hadn't listened to his wife. He hadn't listened to his sons and daughters when his wife had ordered them to convince him of their new family status. Because of getting drunk, he wasn't allowed to enter the house. When drunk, he loudly cursed his eldest son, who had decided to marry the Assamese girl he'd been in love with since the time he'd seen her come out of the classroom next to his. He wasn't antagonistic to the Assamese, and he spoke Assamese like an Assamese man, but the cause was that he was very conservative, and he was afraid of losing his culture he'd carried from East Pakistan as a riot victim. He also mentioned Gunen's failure to find his family despite his strenuous efforts to find them. Given that Gunen had now no roots except what he had at Refugee Gaon, Sujan advised him to escape from the village and not to trust the police, who might come up again and demand more money, which he wouldn't be able to pay unless he borrowed money from Jagat, whose first loan he was still paying at irregular installments—he'd taken that loan to buy four *bighas* of land adjacent to his extra two *bighas* he'd bought from Munda. To steer his mind from the monotony of the thought of the legacy data and the legacy data-related matters, he recalled Meghna and wondered if she'd have compelled him to roam the street of their village or sleep on the veranda of their house if he'd have got drunk like Sujan. But when the thought that he would never have faced such a situation because he would never have got drunk like Sujan or drunk at all, he banished the negativity from his mind. He blamed his habit of drinking on the carpenter. But he never blamed his unfaithfulness to Meghna on Jeuti. Like he'd thought before, he now thought again that the starving libido he'd failed to control was responsible for what had happened to his character for the first and the last time in his life. He mentally thanked the fisherman, whose company had saved him from being a despicable womanizer. They were silently drinking, taking snacks from the platters with their right fingers and placing the snacks on their left palms before tossing them into their mouths. Under the influence of wine, Gunen suddenly burst out crying, calling out to his wife and son and daughter as if they were somewhere within hearing distance. Sujan consoled Gunen while pouring water into the glasses half-filled with wine. The wine glass in his hand close to his lips, Gunen promised, he'd promised many times before, to search and find his family if his body and mind allowed. Gulping down the sip, he found himself in a meditative mood: he wouldn't have discontinued the search unless the NRC problem had robbed him of his precious time and catapulted him into a stage of insanity he could get rid of a little as long as the wine worked in his head. Repeating the same thoughts, stored in his memory, made him feel like living with his family he missed much when alone.

'Wine is not a remedy. And it can never be so,' Gunen said to the night outside.

Sujan neither nodded his head in the affirmative nor in the negative, and so it was apparent that Gunen's philosophy went past his ears, like a fly or a mosquito. Sujan told that he'd always wanted to be happy in his conjugal life, but he thought his wife, his bad luck, had destroyed his happiness, and so, noisily sucking the last drop off his lower lip after putting down the glass, he didn't hesitate to loudly curse his old father, who had forced him to marry her against his mind when he'd promised to marry another girl in the village five kilometres away from theirs.

*

After supper on roti and sabji Gunen had cooked while Sujan had gone on blabbering, they slept on the same bed, driving off mosquitoes by lighting a tortoise brand mosquito repellent coil. As usual, Appon slept under the cot. But in the wee hours, when Gunen opened his eyes to go to the bathroom, he saw Sujan was not in bed, and he searched for him outside the house and didn't find him anywhere. Not spoiling his morning, worrying about where he was, whether he'd gone home, Gunen got into bed, feeling determined to sleep until the streaks of light came into his room, through the crevices of the windows without curtains, but the moment he hugged the pillow Sujan had used, he heard knocks on the door and hurried out of bed to open it and see who the visitor was. He was astonished, seeing Sujan standing on the veranda, the cast net on his left shoulder and a smile characteristic of his friendliness on his lips.

'Get ready. We'll go to catch fish in Taki Beel with this cast net,' Sujan said.

*

After breakfasting on stale roti and tea, they went to Taki Beel, where Sujan had his small fishing boat tied to a tree along with other boats that belonged to other fishermen. No fishermen were there around, because it was just less than half hour past dawn reflecting on the water of the *beel* looking like a small sea the series of small hills overlooking from eastern and southern sides. To its northern side was the Brahmaputra River that submerged the *beel* in the rainy season. The fish came to the *beel* from the river. Its geographical position harboured fish in abundance, and the fish catered to the needs of the villages around and especially to the fishermen, who depended on it for their sustenance. Gunen repeatedly remembering all this whenever he was on the bank of the *beel*.

*

Gunen rowed the boat and Sujan cast the net in the middle of the beel, where he assumed the fish conglomerated. The fish specially conglomerated near hyacinth clusters. Gunen was a good helmsman and a rower.

They fished the *beel* until the sun was on the shoulders of the hills. After fishing was over—they had a good catch of fish—Sujan tied the boat to the tree he'd thought his own since he'd bought the boat from another fisherman.

*

When they came to the market, Sujan gave Gunen a carp fish that weighed around one kilogram. Sujan emptied the creel into a large basket and sat on his stool and started his business. The small fish were alive, and they jumped in the basket. Sujan smoked his *biri* while watching the fish.

The fish in a plastic bag in his hand, Gunen returned home, smoking the *biri* he'd taken from Sujan.

Sitting on the veranda, Appon was waiting for him.

17

At 8:45 pm, Gunen entered his house. He put the bag on the table. The bottle of whisky was in the bag.

After washing his hands and feet, he found two pieces of bread for Appon, reached for the canister on the upper shelf, lifted it down, prised open its mouth with the point of his kitchen knife, and sniffed at the Kit Kat snacks. He took it to his table, placed it near the bottle he'd taken out before going to the bathroom.

He closed the door. He sat down to drink. Sitting on the gunny sack, used as a doormat, Appon was watching him. He gave the pieces to Appon. Appon didn't go out after eating the pieces. Gunen opened the bottle, filled his glass. He took a sip. He drank slowly. He couldn't decide if he should again approach Mr Barman. Whenever he thought of the NRC, he got frightened and confused. Gunen tore a part of the newspaper lying under the cot and offered Appon some snacks when he saw him looking at him, licking his muzzle. He finished the first peg. As he filled the glass, he heard knocks on the door. Mr Barman had perhaps come to say sorry. He hid the bottle and snacks under the cot. The knocks became louder and more frequent. He opened the door and got startled into being speechless after seeing two policemen, who, without his permission, entered the room, wielding their batons to intimidate Appon into stopping barking.

'Appon!' Gunen roared and Appon listened.

Gunen stood still, frightened.

'Are you Gunen Sarkar?' the policeman, who came in first, asked in Assamese.

'Yes,' Gunen answered in Assamese and decided to call them First and Second.

'You were drinking?'

'I'm sorry, sir.'

'You couldn't submit the NRC application. Right?'

'Yes, sir.'

'Why couldn't you do it?'

'I don't have legacy data.'

'Meet the Officer-in-Charge tomorrow without fail. Your name is on the illegal immigrants' list.'

'I can produce all documents except my legacy data.'

'Your documents will be verified at the police station.'

*

The wine took flight from his head. He must find a safe hideout. He folded his mattress, took the essential clothes in a bag, pulled the trunk from under his cot, unlocked it, took out the dagger, and put it in his bag. He took the bottle, empty of two pegs.

He locked the door and stepped into the dirt street, uncertain about when he'd return home or if he'd be able to return home at all. On his head was the trunk, and on his back was the bag. Appon was with him. Would he be able to get the NRC problem solved? He must live in Assam. That was his right. None could snatch away his right. The NRC gave people like him only anxieties. It'd erected walls around him. Now it forced him to leave for an unknown destination. He could walk without difficulty though it was a dark night. The street he'd walked since he'd got off the bus, loaded with refugees, was known to him well. It belonged to him. And he belonged to it. That pleasant feeling of belonging had made him attached to Refugee Gaon and to the vast radius around. He could never even imagine being thrown out. The cool breeze stroked his face. He breathed deeply. His right hand on the trunk, he kept kind of acrobatic balance. Appon sometimes walked ahead; sometimes, behind. The street was dotted with potholes from rain and wind. The bullock carts had caused much damage to the street. Gunen tripped twice. Just after the NRC problem, he'd renew the search for his family. His speed became slow when Tongko Borbora struck his mind. He stopped to look right towards Tongko Borbora's home. He'd visit Tongko Borbora after returning home. Not thinking of anything and not looking in any directions, now he quickly turned the corner to put his feet on the narrow path leading past the banana plantation to Jagat's. Theirs were Assam type houses. The roofs of the houses were of corrugated tin sheets and their walls were of wood and thatched bamboo plastered with sand and cement mixed. They were one of the rich families at Refugee Gaon.

He opened the gate, walked in through the path lined with hedge, and knocked on the door. He knocked a few times. Why no response? Hadn't he returned from the restaurant? Jagat's usual time to return home was between 9.00 to 9:30 pm. The stars said it was past 9.00 pm. Jagat must be home. But why didn't he respond? Was he in the bathroom? Jagat responded to the sixth knock and opened the door.

He hurried past Jagat. After setting the trunk and the bag down on the floor, he sat on the cane chair and took a few deep breaths to regain his energy.

'Why are you here in the night?' Jagat asked, his brows knitted in a frown.

'The police are visiting the houses of the suspected immigrants.' Gunen nervously fingered his hair. 'I'll keep my trunk in your house. I'll hide in a secret place.'

'You may stay with us.'

'I can't. You're my friend.'

'You can go to Majid's or Atin's.'

'They're also my friends.'

'You can go to Munda's.'

'He'll tell the world that I'm hiding in his house when he gets drunk.'

'What about Sujan Das?'

'Just two drinks make him worse than Munda.'

'You're breathing out whisky. You didn't cook, did you?'

'I drank.'

'Now tell me what you're going to do.'

'The police after me. They ordered me to go to the police station. With my documents in the morning. They'll come arrest me. If I don't go. I fear them. Their interrogations upset me. I fear the lock-up. The deportation camps. I'll escape and hide in a safe place.' Gunen glanced at his trunk. 'My trunk will remain in your custody.'

'You look frightened. You look hungry. Go in and wash your hands and mouth. We'll first eat and then decide what you should do or where you should hide.'

'Will you help me?'

'I'm your friend.'

*

'We'll go to the police station tomorrow to settle the case. I think five thousand rupees will be required to settle the case,' Jagat said. 'I'll try to settle it with the help of a sub-inspector. I know him. He's my customer. You'll stay the night here. From here, we'll go to the police station straight. They can't arrest you. You have all documents except the legacy data.'

'Are you sure they can't arrest me?' Gunen asked, a note of anxiety in his voice.

'Trust me.'

'The police are visiting the houses of the refugees. Though the NRC process is going on.'

'The police are responding to the complaints made by some Assamese people. Just a minute.'

Jagat went in and returned with a pack of cigarettes. He sat down, put a rolled paan in his mouth, and lit a cigarette after offering the pack and matches to Gunen. Gunen lit his cigarette after stuffing the paan into his mouth.

Jagat blew the smoke out of his nose. 'Don't worry. I'll give you the money. I think you'd better go back home.'

'Keep the trunk in your room.' Gunen went out. 'Appon, wait a minute. I'll get you rice and chicken meat.'

18

Because of the fear of the police, Gunen had just snatches of sleep. Cocks that crowed in the neighbour's house woke him up. For him it was a very tough situation. He must take the right decision right off. Otherwise, he might be forced to end up in the dungeon of a detention camp before being dumped beyond the Indian border. No guarantee that Jagat would be able to settle the case. Sweat beaded on his forehead. After drying the sweat on his palms, he got up, determined to take the escape route, before dawn.

*

Gunen made four rotis and a cup of tea. With the rotis on a platter and the cup of tea, he came back to his bedroom and sat on his chair while Appon sat near the threshold. They ate rotis together. After eating two rotis, Appon sauntered out, stroking Gunen's legs with his brown tail. Gunen looked at his tail with special attention to its black tip, its special feature Jagat often took a chance to admire. He drank his tea fast. Appon went out.

*

Those two policemen got off their bicycles and came in—no guns or batons in their hands. With his trembling hands,

Gunen pulled the plastic chairs for them, no words coming out of his mouth. They didn't sit down. They told him that he'd better hide in a secret place instead of going to the police station. He thanked the police, humbly bowing down to them. Jagat had settled the case. He thought. He would've felt relieved if the police hadn't told him to hide and if the fear of detention and deportation had totally vanished from his mind.

When the policemen went out and followed the path through the small forest before taking the narrow shortcut towards the police station, he looked up at the sky and let his mind get lost in the patches of clouds moving, creating geometric patterns.

19

Gunen was walking on the veranda when Mr Barman stepped into the compound from nowhere. He offered Mr Barman a smile of welcome into the house. Breathing in the grocery smells coming out of Mr Barman's grocery bag in his right hand, he carefully listened to Mr Barman.

'I'm in a hurry. My wife and children have come from Guwahati.' Mr Barman smiled and licked his lips. 'The NRC has published the Family Tree of all families concerned. I've got your daughter Usha's address. She's married to Sujit Majumdar. They live at Doboka. Meghna and Ginu live at Nagaon. Ginu works as a police sub-inspector. Sujit Majumdar is a banker. Go to Doboka first. Usha will take you to Nagaon.' Mr Barman took a piece of paper from his pants pocket and passed it to Gunen. 'This is the address.'

'Thank you, sir. Thank you so much.'

'Will you now curse the NRC?'

'No, sir. Never.'

'Now this NRC will help you get united with your wife, son, and daughter. It'll help people like you the way they want to be helped. Now no fear of detention camp and deportation. The new law will make the refugees the legal citizens of the country.' Mr Barman glanced at Appon. 'When are you going to Doboka?'

'Day after tomorrow.'

'The sooner, the better.'

Gunen saw him out.

20

By Jagat's Wagon R, Jagat and Gunen arrived at Doboka at 2:55 pm. Jagat had driven his car by NH27.

A young woman came rushing from inside the house as soon as the car stopped in the front yard beside a pond that Gunen assumed to be a fishery. A glance at her face inspired Gunen to compare Meghna's with hers and offer her a smile she hesitantly reciprocated, obviously because he was a stranger. Impatient to confirm that she was none but his daughter he'd been separated from in January 1964, he told her his name and wanted to know if she was Usha. After quenching her curiosity, he introduced Jagat to her, and Jagat got overwhelmed by the respect she showed to him. Gunen kissed her on her forehead, calling to mind the dawn that had sparkled on her golden face delighting the people in the boat.

She led them into the sitting room boasting of the luxury of costly furniture. Gunen and Jagat sat side by side on the sofa.

Usha's elder son, who was a final year engineering student at Assam Engineering College, and her younger son reading science at a higher secondary school, expressed their happiness about meeting their grandfather their mother had remembered to them with elaborate details their grandmother had shared with their mother. They told him that while listening to their mother, they'd only gloomily wondered whether they'd be able to meet their grandfather; they'd worried when they'd seen their grandmother and mother get worried and weep. They were so civilized they showed equal respect to both Gunen and Jagat.

Sujit Majumdar, who was a banker, returned home with mutton and a big carp fish to celebrate the family union—Usha had informed him of their visit, over the phone. Sujit was a tall and handsome guy, not even an ounce of extra fat in his body. The closely cropped beard and moustache matching his face added an attractive dimension to his masculinity. That was maybe one of the reasons why Usha had fallen in love with him. Usha was no less beautiful than her mother. But unlike her mother, she was educated; she'd done her master's in economics at Gauhati University and met Sujit in the same department.

*

There was not much melodrama when Gunen was reunited with Meghna and Ginu. After necessary crying and hugging, they discussed their past and the time when the robbers constrained them to move in different ways and become separated. Gunen told them about how he'd spent his days and nights at Refugee Gaon. All the time, he opened his mouth, he remained conscious of his acts of homicide and debauchery, which he guessed might restrain her from the exuberance of her love and emotions he floated mind in after decades. He let his compunction be washed away by the flood of present happiness.

*

Next afternoon, Meghna, Ginu, and Usha were sitting together on the bed of Ginu's room opposite the garden. Jagat had gone out with Sujit to bring samosa and *jilipi* from the market, where there were many famous sweet shops. Usha liked to eat *jilipi*, like her mother. The thread of the amulet had worn out. Gunen took it off and put it in Meghna's hand. Meghna wanted to know why he was wearing it. He told them about how and why it had come to his arm. Removing the grey hair from her forehead, Meghna asked him to open it and see what there was inside. He used a flat piece of iron to prise it open Ginu had got him from the drawer of his table. He took out the small piece of paper and spread it, holding it with his left and right thumbs and forefingers.

'"ATMABISWAS", Gunen read aloud. 'Self-confidence.' Astonished by their unexpected silence, he threw his inquisitive look at their faces. What was the cause for such behaviour? Was it because he could read and translate ATMABISWAS into self-confidence? Then, to their pleasure, he narrated to them the story about the amulet and about every glorious moment in the house of Tongko Borbora, who had acted as his mentor and teacher. Then, ATMABISWAS in his right palm, he tried to find answers to the question: was Old Gypsy a wise man or a cheat? He would've taken him for a cheat if he'd seen this small piece of paper before. He deleted the question creating doubts in his mind when he thought he'd got benefits from wearing it; it gave him power; it gave him courage. Everyone should wear such an amulet. He put "ATMABISWAS" in the amulet, closed it as before. Then, mentally bowing down to Old Gypsy and promising never to question his wisdom, he tied it to Ginu's arm, like Old Gypsy had tied to his.

'Why do you tie it to my arm, Baba?' Ginu touched the amulet.

'You need it more than me.' Gunen smiled.

'Didn't you miss us, Baba?' Usha asked.

'I'm sure you anxiously searched for us all through the State. You also searched for the cow. We can never forget her. You treated Appon as your friend,' Meghna said.

He told them about how he'd searched for them, how he'd felt in their absence. He looked out the window at the birds flying with happy abandon, beautifying the afternoon sky, before returning to their nests.

'What're you looking at?' Meghna rested her hand on his shoulder.

'The birds. Returning to their nests, with their children. They're happy. They have freedom. They don't require legacy data. Like me. Like a refugee.' Gunen decided to show the fistful of soil to Meghna, Ginu, and Usha.

Black Eagle Books

www.blackeaglebooks.org
info@blackeaglebooks.org

Black Eagle Books, an independent publisher, was founded
as a nonprofit organization in April, 2019. It is our mission
to connect and engage the Indian diaspora and the world at
large with the best of works of world literature published
on a collaborative platform, with special emphasis on
foregrounding Contemporary Classics and New Writing.